NE'ER-DO-WELL

Ne'er-Do-Well

by

Dornford Yates

Dales Large Print Books
Long Preston, North Yorkshire,
BD23 4ND, England.

British Library Cataloguing in Publication Data.

Yates, Dornford
    Ne'er-do-well.

    A catalogue record of this book is
    available from the British Library

    ISBN   978-1-84262-655-9 pbk

Published in Large Print 2009 by arrangement with
Robin Humphreys and Camilla Kirkpatrick,
care of A P Watt Literary, Film and Television Agents

Dales Large Print is an imprint of Library Magna Books Ltd.

Printed and bound in Great Britain by
T.J. (International) Ltd., Cornwall, PL28 8RW

NOTE

Plagiarism is in the air: so I feel that I should make three things plain.

The first is that I do not write, never have written and never shall write any book or article under any name other than my own, prominently displayed. This assurance should give those who know and dislike my work every opportunity of avoiding it. The second is that this is the ninth book of mine in which Richard Chandos appears as the narrator, and the fourth in which Chief Inspector (now Superintendent) Falcon plays a part. The third is that in this, as in all my books, every character and situation has been created and every line has been composed by me alone.

That this book is shorter than my others, I am unhappily aware: but that is how it came out, and I hope and believe that my public would not have wished me to pad the tale.

Perhaps I should add that all the characters, places, occasions and circumstances which I have named or described are wholly imaginary.

DORNFORD YATES

August was in. The sky was cloudless, the sun was agreeably hot, and there was no wind. No sounds but those of Nature came to our ears. The peace was absolute. It was, in fact, an old-fashioned summer's day.

Jonathan Mansel and I were sitting at ease on the terrace, our eyes on the blowing meadows that neighbour my Wiltshire home. My wife was standing between us, with a basket upon her arm.

Jenny seemed young as ever, but the war had aged Mansel, and I was rather less active than I had been before. He had done more than his duty and had justly received a bar to his DSO: but I had had a price on my head and was proud of that. To our content, he came more often to Maintenance than he had come before, 'for the old days hang on here,' he said, 'as nowhere else that I know.'

'I love,' said Jenny, 'to see you two sitting here. You were together the first time we ever met.'

'You told us to go away.'

'I was a little girl then.'

'And we were – rather younger,' I said.

Jenny caught my hand to her heart. Then she stopped to kiss me, let my hand go in silence and moved to the terrace steps.

Without looking back, she went down to the little garden which we were still able to boast. The great Alsatian, Oakham, moved by her side.

'I wish,' I said, 'I wish she wouldn't take it so hard.'

'That's love,' said Mansel. 'But, honestly, William, you carry it off so well that even I, who know you as few men know another, forget that the war put ten years on to your age.'

'When I'm with you – or with Jenny, I forget it myself. And I'm terribly lucky, you know. No false limbs and no disfigurement. And I can still hack.'

'Pain?'

'Nothing to speak of. In the very cold weather, sometimes.'

'Throat?'

'Might be much worse.'

During the war I had paid flying visits to France – by sea and by night. On my last, as I swung myself inboard, I had been hit in the throat.

'After all,' I said, 'I've had a wonderful show. In peace, as in war. Look at the times we had.'

'Yes, they were very good. Remember…'

As always, when we were alone, we began to recall other days. 'Then will he strip his sleeve and show his scars.' So we came back to Jenny, by way of *She Fell Among Thieves*.

'By the mercy of God,' said I, 'she means

no more to Jenny than Charlie Peace. When she killed her daughter's memory, it was the very best deed that Vanity Fair ever did.'

'So it was,' said Mansel. 'God moves in a mysterious way – you can't get away from that. There's Vanity Fair – one of the wickedest women that ever was foaled. Brilliant, treacherous, subtle; completely and utterly ruthless; nothing counting with her but her own desires. Intrigue to Vanity Fair was the breath of life. And here's her daughter, Jenny – Virginia Brooch. The sweetest, gentlest, most artless and loving creature the world has ever known.'

'Jenny's a nymph,' I said. 'When she was eight, her memory was killed. So much we know from her "stand-in". For the next twelve years, under a rough duenna, she lived with Nature alone. Her friends were the streams and pastures, the woods and hills. And all dumb animals. She never had any idea that there was anything else. And then, at twenty, we brought her into the world. If we were to save her life, we couldn't do anything else; but you know, to be honest, she took the change in her stride. Your sister, Jill, was the *dea ex machina*. But, all the same, it was an astonishing thing.'

'Yes,' said Mansel, 'it was. But she is her mother's daughter – don't forget that. And Vanity Fair had poise – an amazing self-possession. And Jenny has it, too. Nothing ruffles Jenny. Look at the war.'

I nodded.

'From all I hear, she was perfectly wonderful. There isn't a farm for miles that doesn't swear by her name. She was at Gauntlet the night that the bombs were dropped and the stables caught fire. Bell said she was like The Pied Piper. The horses just followed her quietly and then stood still in a paddock with her in their midst. And not a head-rope between them.'

Bell appeared with the letters – one for Jenny and two or three for Mansel, sent on from Cleveland Row.

'Bell,' said Mansel, 'who was the biggest felon we ever took on?'

'"Rose" Noble, sir,' said Bell. 'Gedge was dangerous, too. But I was never easy until "Rose" Noble was dead.'

'Bell's right,' said Mansel. 'He'd far more to him than the others. And he had that terrible instinct. Where I feared to assume, he knew.'

'And drive,' said I.

'Yes, he'd a wonderful drive. He'd have had the Hohenems treasure, if we'd been up against him, instead of up against Friar.'

'I'm sure he would,' said I. 'We couldn't have beaten him.'

'Who couldn't you have beaten?' said Jenny, coming out of the library.

'"Rose" Noble, my sweet.'

14

'Well, you did – twice over,' said Jenny.

'I know,' said Mansel, laughing. 'But I never know how we did it.'

To be honest, neither do I.

As I handed my wife her letter–

'Oh, it's from Jill,' she cried.

Jill Pleydell was Mansel's sister, now in Portugal.

Taking her seat on the parapet, Jenny read it aloud.

'DARLING JENNY,

'I'm so glad Jonah's with you. We've just got back from a little place in the South where we bathed all day. Next year you and Richard must come and love it with us. I think the sea-water and sun were very good for Boy's knee. So they would be for Richard. I told you Boy was lecturing at Coimbra: well now Berry's been asked and he's going to do a set on "the English Scene". I think he'll be terribly good. Daphne and Bridget and I are making all the linen for the English "Master's Lodging" that's being built. It's going to be simply lovely – the house, I mean. The Sheres are giving the linen-fold panelling from Feathers, and the Lambournes the dining-room, as it stands, from Sillabub Hall, and the Lyvedens the table silver, beautiful stuff, and the Bagots a Queen Anne bedroom from Chancery. So it will be a real piece of England, won't it? We're all coming over for ten days at the end of September, so you and

15

Richard must come up to London then. Boy and I shall stay for two nights at Lockley, for Nol and Julie are giving what books we like to take. So Boy's going to pick them out of the library. And a Reynolds and one by Gainsborough and one of Crome's. Isn't it splendid of them? I'll let you know when we arrive. Darling Jenny, I want to see you so much. We're very lucky, aren't we, in Richard and Boy? I mean, they are lambs. Please kiss Jonah for me and tell him I love him a million and more than that.

'Your loving
'JILL'

'Like to like,' murmured Mansel.

Jenny went to him and put an arm round his neck.

'For Jill,' she said, and kissed him. 'For darling Jill, who loves you so very much.'

Mansel smiled into her eyes.

'Thank you, my sweet. I'm very fortunate.'

That afternoon we drove to Salisbury, to stroll in the exquisite Close and wonder at the perfect proportions of the Cathedral Church…

The evening was soft and warm, and coffee was served upon the terrace, to our content. For a while we sat there silent, watching the shadows steal upon the landscape and the lovely light of heaven grow slowly dim. The ancient ritual diminished all worldly things.

At length Jenny got to her feet.

'Let's go in,' she said, and turned to the house.

Oakham, her silent familiar, moved in her wake.

A slow wood fire was burning upon the library's hearth, and the three of us sat down about it, more grateful for its presence than conscious of its warmth.

When we had talked for an hour, I rose, passed to a table, poured Jenny barley-water and asked Mansel what he would like.

'Barley-water, William.'

'You mean that?' I said.

'I do.'

I drank it, too. Had I been offered champagne, I would have turned it down. The age of champagne was over. And beer as well.

As I set his glass by his side–

'We've had our day,' I said.

'Yes,' said Mansel, and smiled. 'But what a day, William!'

'It suited me,' I said.

'And me. The open air, and doing something worth while. "And gentlemen in England, now a-bed…" D'you know what I value most?' I shook my head. 'That our names were respected and feared in *The Wet Flag*.'

I laughed.

'How many people today would value that?'

'Not very many,' said Mansel. 'Times have changed, and the world that we knew has

17

gone. Matters of life and death are not quite nice. Many subscribe in spirit to the price the Boche put on your head.'

'That,' said Jenny, 'is because in their hearts they're afraid.'

Mansel nodded.

'I fear that's the true explanation, look at it how you will.'

The next was a fine, brave day, with the faintest breeze and hardly a cloud in the sky: and so, with one consent, we made an excursion which not everyone would have liked. Taking our luncheon with us, we drove by country lanes to The Stukely Walks. And when I say 'drove', I mean it. With Jenny and Oakham beside him, Mansel drove the gig; and I drove the dog-cart, with Carson sitting beside me and Bell behind. It was a pretty progress: we only encountered six cars. We took two hours to cover the fifteen miles. But we saw the countryside as the countryside should be seen – as our fathers and grand-fathers saw it, and felt refreshed. The Walks we had to ourselves – they are off the map. Carson and Bell were ravished: I really believe that the horses enjoyed it, too. We had brought a bucket and feeds, and the servants took off their harness and let them roll. I drove the gig back, and Jenny sat by my side, her beauty flushed with her pleasure in every mile. Her enjoyment was so infectious, I found the leisurely journey far too short. So we came back to Maintenance, just as a sinking sun was gilding the oaks and elms and casting giant shadows upon the grateful meadows, freckled with sheep. Calling back Time, we had stolen a summer's day.

The next day, Sunday, we lunched at Buckram Place. All three of us could remember when this had been maintained as a stately home – the home of, say, forty people, high and low. But now there were only four. The splendid gardens, which had given great pleasure to thousands throughout the summer months, the splendid gardens were gone, and the meadows ran up to the house. The lodges and cottages were empty – 'We'd let them for next to nothing, but people say that they're too far from a town.' The stables lodged two horses; the coach-houses kept two serviceable cars and a truck. The whole of the house was shut, except for four rooms – library, withdrawing-room, kitchen and servants' hall. Natalie and her husband lived and ate in the library, slept in the drawing-room. Their working butler and cook used the kitchen and servants' hall. Two bathrooms had been installed to serve these 'suites'. Somehow husband and wife maintained the estate. The sheep, the cattle, the crops – these things made up their life.

'We don't make a farthing,' said Baldric. 'In fact, we're down on the deal. But that is because we do as has always been done. Happily, it doesn't matter. As long as our capital lasts, we can live upon that. And the farms must have the best. They call us the bloated rich. I'd like to see one of them do the weekday's work we do. We think ourselves lucky if we've only a ten-hour day – and that, for nothing at all, except our *amour propre*. Give me democracy.'

'Now, now,' said Natalie.

'You make me ashamed,' said I.

'Don't be absurd, Richard. You have been shot to pieces.'

'Eleven wounds,' said Jenny. 'I don't know why he's alive.'

'Now, now,' said I. 'I get along very well. And our two farms are very easy to run.'

'We live,' said Mansel, 'at an unfortunate time. We've seen the great days pass and the pinchbeck days come in. That's always a sorry spectacle. Plenty of Romans felt as we do, you know. And then the last crash came, and the dark ages supervened.'

'That'll learn 'em,' said Baldric.

'Yes,' said Mansel, 'it will. Free wigs will be off. As for a forty-hour week, whoever wants to survive will have to fight for his life – for three or four hundred years.'

'The pansy,' I said, 'the pansy won't like being learned. He'll probably ring up the police.'

'No doubt,' said Mansel drily. 'But he will

get no reply.'

'We must go down,' said Natalie, 'with everything "all correct".'

'That's right,' said Jenny. 'We feel exactly the same.'

I nodded.

'One's house in order, hay carried, animals watered and fed. Of course it won't matter at all, except to us.'

'And why,' said Natalie. 'Why will it matter to us?'

'Self-respect,' said Mansel. 'We're all the same. If I were told that I was to die at four, I should arise at three, to bathe and shave. But I have a feeling that this time we shan't be warned.'

'In the twinkling of an eye?' said Baldric.

'That's my belief.'

Baldric frowned.

'And the roof of Odd Acre's new barn is only half on.'

'I think you'll have time for that. I don't think it's coming just yet. I may be wrong, of course. It may come tonight. But somehow I don't think it will. But when it comes, I think it'll come in a flash.'

'And fall upon us?' said Jenny.

'Yes, my sweet. Get us, and they've got the lot. Wipe England out, and the rest will be at their disposal.'

Baldric nodded.

'Machines do not a warrior make.'

21

'Nor boasts a man-at-arms.'

Mansel continued, smiling.

'And we're painfully vulnerable. But, as I've said, I don't think it's coming just yet. I've nothing to go on, of course.'

'But it's bound to come?' said Natalie.

'That's my belief,' said Mansel. 'America will almost certainly turn the switch. Trip over the wire, if you like. But the dump is there, waiting. The end of this civilization is overdue. We've flouted the laws of Nature for several years. As for the laws of God...'

'Jonah,' said Baldric, 'I'm with you all the way. Nine of the ten Commandments are simply ignored today. The only one honoured is the second – which people can't be bothered to break.'

'And we can do nothing,' said Natalie.

'We can go on behaving. I can't think of anything else.'

'An Act of God,' said I, 'could stop the rot.'

'It could, indeed – if its effects were wholesale. They would have to be so crippling that over-civilization would go by the board. So there's really not much in it. We've got to get back to the laws of God and of Nature. When the world obeys those laws, the world will be happy again.'

With that, we left the house, to return to husbandry: for our pleasant host and hostess drove us about the estate. During the tour, my admiration for the Baldrics rose very high. Only devotion to duty could have produced such results – a very rare devotion; but that was theirs. And men and beasts were plainly so pleased to see them wherever they went. Let me at once admit that without their inherited wealth they could not have so maintained the Buckram estate: but when it is remembered that they could, had they pleased, have kept a most handsome home and have led a luxurious life, I think it does them great credit that they would not so much as employ a deputy.

As we drove back to Maintenance–

'More meat for the demagogues,' said Mansel. 'You see, they're landed gentry. That they work like galley-slaves is beside the point. They are the master and mistress of Buckram Place.'

'That's Communism,' said Jenny.

'All demagogues,' said I, 'are convertible Communists.'

'How d'you convert them, darling?'

'Make them landed gentry,' said I. 'But I don't think they'd live in two rooms at Buckram Place.'

The Earl and Countess of Avon drove over to luncheon with us on the following day.

They were a gentle pair. Nol Avon was more than half blind from a wound in the first great war: it was Julie's pride and plea-sure to lend her husband her eyes. To see them together was moving – each loved the other so well. For the last few years, except to visit close friends, they seldom moved outside their beautiful Hampshire home. I except their visits to Canada, where Avon had a fine ranch.

'I'm ashamed of you, Nol,' said Mansel. 'Stripping Lockley like this.'

Nol Avon laughed.

'For the Master's Lodging, you mean? We're not giving very much. Besides, the stuff will go to a very good home. What is the sense of keeping it to be sold?'

'Oh, I know,' said Mansel. 'Have you really made Boy free of your beautiful library?'

'Jonah, as you probably saw, six months ago old Raven of Maidenhair died. When his library came to be sold, a dealer measured the shelves with a three-foot rule – and purchased those handsome volumes at so much a yard.'

'My God,' said I.

'It's true,' said Nol. 'And we're sentimental enough to feel that such fine and faithful servants shouldn't be treated like that.' He sighed. 'The children should be all right. They're taking to Canada. Not what I'd hoped, of course. But I think it's best. And we shall get through somehow… The staff and the tenants are safe – I've seen to that. It's best to do these things while yet there is time. And the Public Trustee has been extremely

24

helpful. The Income Tax people are cross, but we've nothing to hide. We've been living on the family silver for more than a year.'

'O wise Lord Avon,' said Mansel.

'Say rather "prudent", Jonah.'

'Or *méchant*,' said Julie. 'Quand on l'attaque, il se défend.'

'Very good,' cried Jenny, clapping her hands. 'You'll be known as the wicked Lord Avon in days to come.'

'To that, my sweet, I am prepared to submit. And you, Richard?'

'We're living on capital, too. If we weren't, we shouldn't be here. Nor would the staff. And they don't want to leave Maintenance. Of course we don't hunt any more, but we do what we can with the farms and I think we shall just make out.'

'And Berry and Daphne, Jonah?'

'They can't come back,' said Jonah. 'Berry would never survive a winter here. He's quite all right by Lisbon. And Jill and Boy won't leave them. I'm very thankful to winter there myself.'

'How wise you were to make over White Ladies when you did.'

'It broke our hearts,' said Mansel, 'but we felt it was right.'

'And that will survive; but Maintenance, Lockley and Buckram will disappear. I don't like the present much: but I like the look of the future a good deal less.'

Mansel nodded. 'In twenty or thirty years, the process of levelling down will be complete. That is, if no catastrophe occurs. Nothing worth having will be left. There'll be no one and nothing to look up to, no examples to follow, nothing whatever to strive for except existence itself. Life will be painfully dull. And those in power will treat all the others like dirt. And then, after much tribulation and many years, the great days will come again.'

'The price of equalization,' said Nol, 'is painfully high.'

There was a little silence.

'I remember,' said I, 'the first time I saw White Ladies...'

On the following morning, Tuesday, Mansel and I were in the coach-house, considering the dog-cart and gig.

'Not many left,' said Mansel. 'And there used to be thousands. I suppose they were all dismantled or broken up.'

'The gig came from Cockrow,' I said. 'I bought it through Shere, when old Lord Scarlet died. It was George that got the dog-cart – I can't remember where.'

'And as good as new,' said Mansel. 'They built stuff that lasted then. The broughams, too! What exquisite things they were.'

Jenny came stepping across the stable-yard.

'Darling,' she said, 'Beecham's rung up

26

from Clarion, to ask if I'll come.'

Beecham was a very good vet.

'If its Adamant,' I said, 'you're not going. I've only one wife.'

Mansel looked at me, and Jenny put a hand to her mouth.

'Who's Adamant?' said Mansel.

I sighed.

'Adamant,' said I, 'is a stallion. He's Colin Delaney's pet. But for Adamant's temper, he might have made a great name: but he does very well as a sire. The trouble is he's a rogue. And when the fit is on him, he's really dangerous. He's damned near killed one lad and he's maimed another for life.'

'I know,' said Jenny, 'I know. But he is such a lovely fellow. I know he goes off the deep end, but that's only because he's so terribly highly strung. Come with me, darling, and tell me what I may do.'

All three of us drove to Clarion, a very pleasant establishment, sunk in the downs.

As I brought the car to a standstill, Colin Delaney came forward, with Beecham behind.

'What's the trouble, Colin?' I said.

'It's his eye,' said Colin. 'It's shut and weeping and sending him out of his mind. The trouble is, of course, he won't let us look.'

'He's got something in it,' said Beecham. 'It may be only a seed. But you know what Adamant is. I can't get anywhere near him.

27

As for everting the eyelid...'

He threw up his hands.

'Let me talk to him,' said Jenny.

'Very well,' said I. 'But please don't ask me to let you go into his box.'

'I wouldn't let her,' said Colin.

The five of us made our way to Adamant's box.

The upper leaf of the stable-door was open: when we peered cautiously in, a truly pitiful picture met our eyes. The embodiment of defiance, the magnificent black was standing with his quarters to the opposite wall. His glorious head was up, and he made me think of some warrior facing death. His right eye was flaming – there is no other word. But the left was closed and twitching, and tears were steadily trickling over his jowl. As Jenny came up to the door, I moved directly behind her, holding her body lightly under the arms and ready to throw her in an instant to right or left. At a nod from me, Colin Delaney and Beecham stood, one upon either side, all ready to catch my wife. Mansel was a little behind us, standing perfectly still. And so we all stood in silence for two or three minutes or more.

Then–

'Why, Adamant,' said Jenny: 'I've come to help you out. I got a fly in my eye about a month ago, and it hurt like anything. I couldn't get it out – that's one of the things that no one can do for himself. But Richard got it out for me, and then I was quite all right. Come here, old fellow, and let me have a look.'

In this strain she spoke to the horse, as though he were an acquaintance, recalling other occasions on which they had met; and after five or six minutes Adamant moved very slowly up to the open leaf.

Nobody moved a muscle, as his head came out of the box.

Then Jenny put up her sweet face, and the stallion poked his head, blew on her once or twice and then nuzzled her brow with his lips.

Jenny took his head in her hands...

Twenty-five minutes later, she picked a stubborn hayseed from under the upper lid.

Then she sponged the eye with warm boracic water which Mansel had brought, and, speaking very gently, told Adamant that all would be well.

'You've been simply splendid,' she said. 'I know how dreadful it is to have one's eyelid lifted: and yet you stood like a rock. And now you'll have your reward. I expect that now it feels as though it's still there: that's always the way: but in five or six minutes you'll find that that lovely eye of yours is as good as new. And now goodbye, old fellow. I'll come back and see you soon.'

With her hands about his muzzle, she

kissed the velvet nose.

As I drew her back into safety–

'He's been through a lot,' she said. 'D'you think, Mr Beecham, he might have a quart of beer?'

'I think so,' said Beecham, weakly. He wiped the sweat from his face. 'To be perfectly frank, I could do with a drink myself.'

I never drink champagne in the daytime, but that day I broke my rule. Colin was most insistent. Besides, of course, I had to drink Jenny's health. And to be as honest as Beecham, it helped me up.

Sitting in the library that evening, Mansel regarded his palms.

'What I witnessed this morning,' he said, 'makes our exploits seem rather thin.' He looked at me. 'I don't blame you for letting her do it, for no man has the right to withhold a miracle. But–'

'Jonathan, darling,' said Jenny, 'there wasn't any danger, once Adamant knew it was me.'

'I know, I know,' said Mansel. 'Still, if he'd thrown up his head … no more than that…' He put a hand to his eyes. 'Well, William knows what I mean.'

'By God, I do,' said I. I took Jenny's hand in mine. 'You see, my darling, you're rather precious to us, and to let you hob-nob with violence shakes us up. Never mind. Let's talk about – well, Shapely.'

Mansel shook his head.

'Shapely was no more a crook than Crippen was. But he had a powerful motive for what he did. Of that, he made no secret – he pointed it out to the police. But his alibi was cast iron – or so he thought. The murderer always has a motive: the crook's is usually obvious; the man he kills is the man who embarrasses or has witnessed his commission of felony: he rarely kills out of spite. If he's an able crook, he's very much harder to get, for he knows all the tricks of the trade. Just look at the runs which the men we've been talking of had. "Rose" Noble, Gedge, Brevet; Pharaoh, The Shepherd and Forecast; Barabbas and Friar: they'd all been at it for years and all were murderers.'

'And the police couldn't deal with them?' said Jenny.

'Our police were weighted out by restrictions and rules: the continental police made next to no effort to get them. Take *The Wet Flag* in Rouen: the place was a blasted scandal: that café became so exclusive that no one, who wasn't a crook, could go in – and come out alive. Yet it was never raided, much less closed. For that, there was no excuse, for the French police are not hampered as are the English police.

'In the old days in London – say, seventy years ago – every three months the police would raid Seven Dials, a well-known resort of ruffians of every kind: and they'd round up all the men into Bow Street Police Station's yard. There pulpits had been set up. In the pulpits were plain-clothes men. And they would look the crowd over and pick out the wanted men. All these were detained; and the rest were told to get out. And they went in gratitude, thanking the police at the gates and touching their hats; for all were guilty of something and feared that their hour was come.

'Now that reminiscence is true: and it's typical of the freedom the English police enjoyed. But now they can't do that. If they did, on the following morning they'd be served with writ after writ for false imprisonment – and that, by the scum of the earth; and questions would be asked in the House; and the Commissioner would have to resign. The Continental Police have great freedom, but they show no initiative. They'll kill a dead case all right, but, when a case is alive, they don't go after their man.

'In spite of their many handicaps, I think the English police do extremely well. They're wonderfully quick off the mark, nothing is too much trouble and they never let go. We both know Falcon – I know him very well. He always was outstanding. He could, I am sure, had he pleased, have been an Assistant Commissioner years ago. But he'll have to retire before long. And when he does, he will be a terrible loss.'

'He lunched with us,' said Jenny, 'about six months ago.'

I nodded.

'He just drove up to the house and asked if we'd give him lunch, "Stay the night," said I, "and we'll give you a bed." "I wish I could," says he; "but I've got to get on." He was plainly terribly tired, and we made him lie down after luncheon and rest till four. That he should have turned to us did me a lot of good.'

'I rather fancy,' said Mansel, 'that Falcon felt the same.'

'He thanked us so sweetly,' said Jenny. 'When he was leaving, he took my hand in both his. Then he said, "Mrs Chandos, there are only two doors in England at which, if I needed comforting, I should knock. And the other door hangs in Cleveland Row."'

'It's nice to know that,' said Mansel. 'Falcon means what he says.'

'Talk of the Devil,' they say…

Be that as it may, the very next afternoon Bell came in to say that Superintendent Falcon was on the telephone.

'Chandos here, Superintendent.'

'Six months ago, Mr Chandos, you gave me a generous inch. Now I am taking an ell. Will you be so very kind as to lodge me for two or three nights?'

'With very great pleasure, Superintendent.'

'I shan't be an ordinary guest, for I'm on the job. Out and about all day. My men will manage all right at *The Crown* at Ne'er-do-well: but it's going to be rather more crowded than I should like.'

'Arrive when you please. Your room will be ready and waiting in half an hour. We're all alone, except for Colonel Mansel.'

'What more can I ask? Goodbye.'

When I told the others, Jenny clapped her hands and dashed off to prepare a room and Oakham ran barking behind her and Mansel began to laugh.

'O fortunate Falcon!' he said. 'And where is Ne'er-do-well?'

'Some ten miles off. It used to be rather nice, but it's more of a bus-stop now than anything else.'

'What brings him there, I wonder?'

'I can't imagine,' said I. 'It must be important, though, for him to come down.'

'Highly important,' said Mansel. 'Never mind. We're going fishing. Sufficient unto the hour is the richness thereof.'

I was never much of an angler, although I enjoy the pursuit: and if my surroundings are fair, I get as much pleasure of them as I do of the taking of fish. Which means, of course, that I am not a fisherman born, as Mansel is. Still, though my catch was nothing, I recall with infinite pleasure that Wednesday afternoon.

The water was retired and private, and we were the only people to move by its precious banks. A slowly moving mirror, it rendered all that it captured as never did glass, refining the gold of the sunshine, clothing with mystery the shadows and making magic out of the sway of a leaf. Jenny lay still between us, watching the life of the stream, and Oakham lay couched beside her, his eyes on her eager face. The turf was so fine and verdant, the neighbouring woods were so full, the air was so sweet-smelling, and the pattern of light and shade so ancient and so rare. 'Now came still evening on...'

In the last twenty minutes Mansel landed two trout, but I had nothing to show when we made our way home.

Whilst we were changing, Falcon drove up to the door. But Bell took him up to his room, while Carson took charge of his car.

'Have I time for a bath, Bell?'

'Certainly, sir. I'll turn it on before I lay out your clothes.'

'I've no dress-clothes with me.'

'The mistress said you were not to think about that.'

That was as much as I heard, but Falcon was very quick and came in, looking very nice, as cocktails were served.

We naturally asked no questions, and he never mentioned his business till dinner was over and done. And then, in the library,

Falcon opened his mouth.

'I know that you'll keep my counsel, so, if you would like to hear, I'm going to tell you what I've been doing today. It's a great relief to me to be able to talk.'

Jenny spoke for us all.

'It's very nice of you to put it that way.'

I glanced at the open windows and got to my feet.

'Perhaps you're right,' said Falcon.

Before I could ring–

'Oakham, darling,' said Jenny, 'will be even better than Bell.'

'So he will,' I said.

Jenny led Oakham to the windows.

'Guard the terrace, Oakham: and growl if anyone comes.'

The great dog nosed her hand and then lay down on the sill.

Falcon looked at me.

'Wainscot Hall, Mr Chandos. You know the place?'

'Three miles from Ne'er-do-well. I know it by sight. It used to belong to the Barhams. Then a convent bought it and made it a nursing-home.'

'A very exceptional Home?'

'I've heard so and I can believe it. A nun's interpretation of duty is usually very fine.'

'I imagine it's hard to get into.'

'So I'm told.'

'Did you know Lord St Amant was there?'

36

I shook my head.

St Amant was a fine fellow, and very popular. Born in 1919, he first, so to speak, hit the headlines in 1941. He had been reported killed in the retirement on Dunkirk. He should have been listed as 'missing, believed killed'; but a gunner, later killed on the beaches, had declared that he died in his arms, and such was the prevailing confusion that the wrong report was made. Fourteen months later, he had walked into the British Embassy at Lisbon. So he rose from the dead. He was at that time the Hon. Joris Eyot, his father's only son. He had succeeded to the title in 1945. As Lord St Amant, horses made up his life. He had won four Classic races and had ridden in the National twice. A personal friend of Royalty, a very good-looking man, his invariably debonair manner delighted the public's heart. He was a bachelor.

'I know him slightly,' said Mansel. 'He's a most exceptional man. The very mould of good form.'

'Was,' said Falcon. 'He was found dead this morning at six o'clock. An operation was performed on his jaw exactly a week ago. He was in excellent health and recovering fast. In these circumstances, the House Surgeon naturally declined to give a death-certificate. More. As a result of a communication which he felt it was his duty to make to the police, the Chief Constable saw the wisdom of calling us in at once: and I arrived at the Home at eleven o'clock today.

'As you will believe, the position is delicate. The dead man is not only a peer, but an eminent sportsman and a favourite with high and low. The Home is a Convent Home and above reproach. The inevitable publicity will be for the Sisterhood a dreadful ordeal. But the Law must take its course, and if we can do it, Justice has got to be done.'

Mansel drew in his breath.

'I don't envy you, Falcon,' he said. 'You're on a shocking bad wicket, and that's the truth.'

'I realize this,' said Falcon. 'The atmosphere alone puts you off your game. It's so embarrassing. I feel I'm a trespasser – as of course I am. I belong not only to the world which these holy women have renounced, but to a part of that world which women who are not nuns are taught to avoid. I'm not going to say they're hostile: but I have to keep my distance. And that doesn't help a policeman to get at the truth.

'I saw the House Surgeon first. He was there to meet me, when I got out of the car. He was summoned at six o'clock from his house in the grounds. By St Amant's night-sister. He arrived in ten minutes' time. The peer had been dead for two hours, but not more than four. He had seen him the evening before at eight o'clock. He was then in excellent form and looking forward to leaving in two days' time.

'"I'm told," said I, "that you think his lordship was poisoned."

'The fellow looked rather worried.

'"I knew that was coming," he said. "I'm afraid I spoke out of turn."

'"I don't agree," said I. "But why do you think he was poisoned?"

'"Well," he said, "of course I examined the body without delay. No marks at all. But – well, there was something about his expression which was not natural. When you see it," he added, "you'll see what I mean."

'"Heart?" said I.

'"Sound as a bell. He was one of the fittest men I've ever seen."

'"The room's under guard?"

'"Yes, there's a constable there."

'"It was you that rang up the police?"

'"Yes. The police-surgeon came along soon after eight. While he was here, orders came through to touch nothing until you arrived."

'We'd been talking on the steps. As we entered the hall, a nun came out of a lodge.

'The doctor said who I was, and the nun just lowered her head and turned away.

'As we moved to a corridor–

'"Will you take me to see the Mother Superior first?"

'The man hesitated. Then–

'"Perhaps you're right," he said. "Will you come this way?"

'My reception was very cold. However, I said my piece and gave what assurances I could. She heard me out in silence. Then–

'"I'm told," she said, "that an Inquest will be held."

'"I'm afraid that's so."

'"Understand this. I cannot and will not allow any sister here to attend."

'"Madam," said I, "that is not a matter for me. The Coroner will summon whom he wishes to come to his Court."

'"But he'll listen to you, Superintendent."

'I saw my chance and jumped in.

'"His word is law, madam: but he will decide whom to summon upon the report of the police. The more help the police are given the more help they are happy to give. I can't say more than that."

'"You will please recommend that none of the sisters are called."

'"I can't promise that. I think his lordship's night-sister will certainly have to appear."

'"And if I refuse to release her?"

'"That, madam, will be a matter for the Coroner. But if it is publicity which you desire to avoid, I can only tell you that such a refusal would treble the publicity which such a case must receive." The woman's temper was rising: for all her icy calm, I knew that one of her feet was tapping the floor. So I

40

thought it best to speak out. "And now please let me say this. So grave a matter as this cannot be hushed up. Lord St Amant has died a mysterious death. I am here to find out who or what caused that death. You will receive from me the utmost consideration: but that I should not swerve from my duty is as much to your interest as mine, for it must never be thought that your House has something to hide." That brought her up to her feet: so I went on at once. "And now, by your leave, the doctor will show me the room."

'With that, I bowed and left her, and the House Surgeon followed me out.

'As we came to the door of the room—

'"I think," he said, "that I ought to tell you this. First, to the Mother Superior the utter seclusion of her flock means more than life itself. Secondly, several of the sisters used to bear well-known names. The night-sister in question was a famous society beauty some years ago.'

'"Oh, dear," said I. "Do patients recognize her?"

'"That, I can't say."

'Then he unlocked the door, and we entered the room. French windows, which were wide open, gave to a terrace exactly as these do here, and a constable, standing outside, looked round to see who it was. He had been warned to expect me, so all was well.

'I'll give you the layout now.

'Six rooms in a row, all giving on to a terrace rather wider than yours. Broad steps, like yours, leading down into meadows, and, four hundred yards away, a country road. At either end of the terrace a wing of the house, so that the terrace is sheltered, except from the South. These rooms are reserved for male patients. In the recent hot weather the windows have stood wide open, day and night.

'When I looked at the dead man's face, I saw at once what Dr Paterson meant. It wore a look of something more than surprise. It looked as though he had felt some strange sensation for which he could not account – and in that moment had died. His arms were bent and his hands were drawn up, palm downward upon the bed, as though he'd meant to raise himself up. But he hadn't had time.

'I looked at Paterson.

'"He was asleep and woke to find his life ebbing."

'"That's the impression I have."

'I went over the room. It was easy enough to inspect, as you will believe. Very simple, very clean. On the table beside the bed were a bell-push, a novel, a box of cigarettes, a lighter, a glass half full of water, and a dessert-spoon.

'I asked the doctor what the spoon was for.

'"Probably," he said, "for tablets. Of the nature of aspirin. No patient is given the bottle, but two or three tablets would be placed in the bowl of the spoon."

'"Was he taking tablets?" I said.

'"Yes. He still had pain, and it used to wake him up."

'"I see. Was the pain severe?"

'"Oh, no. But enough to keep him awake, unless relieved."

'"Was the bone diseased?"

'"No, it was perfectly healthy. For no apparent reason a cyst had formed. That had to be cut out, or, sooner or later, the jaw would have broken in two. Spontaneous fracture, we call it. If it's properly done, the bone soon grows again."

'"Please tell me about these tablets you said he might have."

'"They're the latest thing, and they're called japonica. We use them all the time. They're harmless and swift in action. They have no ill effects."

'"Could a number be fatal?"

'"Perhaps, if you took about thirty and had a weak heart. But the sister will only give them every two hours."

'"Any possibility of mistake?"

'"None. All dangerous drugs are locked in a plate-glass case of which I have the key."

'I sent the constable off to bring the photographers in: and when they had done, all the stuff on the table was treated for fingerprints.

'While this was being done, the House

Surgeon went away. He had things to attend to, of course, and patients to see.

'I walked out on to the terrace and, presently, down the steps. I stood there looking all round, for you never know. And then I saw a tablet, lying to the right of the steps. I was very lucky to see it, for the grass was three inches long: but the tablet had lodged halfway through. I sought high and low for another, without success. That tablet's in London now. I can't believe it will yield any finger-marks, but at least tomorrow morning I shall be told what it is.'

'That's one of the tablets,' said I, 'which the night-sister put in the spoon?'

'I think so. They were taken away, and others were put in their place. Whether anyone saw me find it, I do not know. I've mentioned it to Rogers, but nobody else.

'Soon after that, the local superintendent arrived, and the police-surgeon with him. They had an ambulance with them. Paterson returned, and the body was taken away. (The two did the post-mortem together this afternoon. Portions of certain organs are being analysed now.)

'There was a built-in wardrobe. Inside were the dead man's clothes and other personal effects. A chequebook, a note-case, a gold wrist-watch, a small bunch of keys.

'I turned to Paterson.

'"By your leave," I said, "I shall take

44

charge of these. And if the clothes can be packed, I'll take them with me when I go."

"'I'll see to that, Superintendent. By the way, he was wearing a ring."

"'I know. Please take it off this afternoon."
'Then I asked about the night-sister.

"'She's resting now," said Paterson. "She should be asleep."

"'What time does she come on duty?"

"'At eight o'clock."

"'Can I see her at three?"

"'I can't say yes, Superintendent. The Mother Superior can."

"'I understand. Now, of the six rooms here, I see this is Number Four. Who is in Three and Five?"

"'The patient in Number Three is in a very bad way. He's kept under morphia most of the time."

"'I see. And Five?"

"'He's quite fit to be seen. A highly intelligent fellow. Rather sardonic humour. Man of the world."

"'May I know what he's here for?"

"'Operation on his knee. Delayed result of a car smash a year or two back."

"'Capable of walking?"

"'Oh, no."

"'Lord St Amant could walk?"

"'Oh, yes. I know that he strolled on the terrace yesterday afternoon. I believe he went in and saw Dallas."

45

'"Dallas is Number Five?"

'"Yes."

'"Can I see him in five minutes' time?"

'"I'll arrange that at once."

'I gave certain instructions to Rogers and asked the local superintendent to police both gates, for I knew that by then the Press would be on the way. And I asked him to let them know that I'd see them at half past six.'

'You always do that,' said Mansel.

'I find it pays.

'Then I walked up to the windows of Dallas' room.

'"At last,' he said. "Superintendent Falcon, I think. Kenelm Dallas, at your service. I've awaited your arrival with impatience. Pray sit down in that very uncomfortable chair. Austerity is the watchword in convents today. It was not always so. If we may believe – but I stray from the matter in hand."

'I sat down in the chair and accepted a cigarette.

'"With impatience?" I said.

'"Oh, don't let me raise your hopes. I have but a button to put in the offertory bag. I fear that's a solecism. Offertory is a noun."

'"I don't despise buttons," I said.

'"All in good time. And now please question me."

'"You knew that Lord St Amant was in the room next to you?"

'"Not until yesterday. But he was 'walking

46

wounded', which I am not. And as he was passing those windows, I called to him. And so he came in and sat down. A very pleasant fellow – I wish I'd met him before. He promised to look me up next time he visited Paris. I live in France, you know. The service is more expensive, but just as good as it was. And if the money is there, the French are far too shrewd to troy with *Egalité*."

'"Who told you that he was dead?"'

'"Paterson. A steady, dutiful man, as no doubt you've observed. Tea is always brought to me round about six o'clock."'

'"By the night-sister?"'

'"Yes. This morning it didn't appear. Instead, I heard goings and comings, and those, in haste. Then somebody must have felt faint, for Paterson spoke from the terrace – 'Let her sit on the steps and see that she holds her head down.'

'"I rang then and at last a strange sister appeared. I desired to see Paterson at once. After two or three minutes he came and told me St Amant was dead. 'What of?' said I. 'I don't know.' And then he was gone.

'"Well, that gave me food for thought. It meant, of course, an Inquest, and there was a kettle of fish. Great pressure would be put upon Paterson – to which, I was perfectly sure, he would never yield – to sign a certificate. Dracona would kick with cold fury against the pricks. Sister Helena would be distraught. That's the night-sister – a very attractive girl, as you will agree."

"'I haven't seen her yet."

"'A pleasure to come. She's going to be your star turn. At the Inquest, I mean. My God, what a film this would make! Well, the day-sister brought my breakfast, which is the night-sister's job. She's older and level headed. Not even a hydrogen bomb would throw her out of her stride. Sister Geneviève. I looked at her and smiled. "Is Sister Helena better?" She looked at me very hard. Then, "I think so. She's lying down." "I'm very sorry," I said, "about everything." "Pray for us all," she said: and with that, she was gone. Then the local police arrived – I saw them upon the terrace: they came that way. So I had fresh food for thought."

"'What did you think about?"

"'Murder," said Dallas. "Till then, the question of murder had never entered my head. And so I began to cast back...

"'I nearly always wake about four o'clock. The pain seems to call me then. So I take two japonica tablets, and after a little I go to sleep again. St Amant told me it was the same with him. This particular spot must receive some broadcast of Nature's about that time. Say rosy-fingered dawn is taking her bath. Last night I woke as usual, but when I switched on my light, I saw it was a quarter to two. Well, I didn't think much about it, but I took my tablets and went to sleep again."

"'Pain?'

"'Nothing to speak of. But I thought that if I took them, I might not wake again. Nor I did – till nearly six.

"'Well, there's my button, Superintendent. Something woke me up at a quarter to two. A footfall, perhaps. I don't know."

"'Windows wide open?'

"'Yes. Often enough the sisters come in that way."

"'And that is all you remember?'

"'All I remember – yes. But I have a definite feeling that there was something else. Some impression that I received. But I cannot recapture it."

"'When you say impression...'

"'That's as near as I can get – for the moment. I have a feeling that I was aware of something."

"'Something unusual?'

"'I can't go as far as that. It may have been nothing of importance – the rustle of a habit, for instance."

"'I understand. If it should return to your mind...'

"'You shall have it at once."

'We talked for a few minutes more, when I took my leave.

'I saw the day-sister next. She is a notable woman: and, as Dallas said, of a type that nothing could shake. If only she'd been on

49

night duty… I mean, there's a witness for you. No Coroner's Court would faze her. Reserved, of course, but natural. But she, of course, was off duty. The Sisters have their own quarters at the back of the house. When she bade St Amant goodnight, he was in excellent form. St Geneviève, he called her. When she protested, "Come, come," he said; "between saints…"

"'I think," I said, "that he had all the virtues."

"'You knew him, Superintendent?"

"'Unhappily, only by repute. And sight, of course. I've seen him many a time."

"'He was the sort of man that other men die for, Superintendent. I can see any one of his servants giving his life for his. I'd only known him a week, but I would have done so gladly – without a thought. He was incomparable."

'I made no answer to that – I didn't know what to say. After such a tribute as that, any condolences would have been out of place. Besides, she was very near tears.

'After a little, I asked if he had had visitors. So far as she knew, none. Letters? She had seen none. After all, he was only in for eight days. Pain? Not very much after the first two days. He never complained. Talked a lot of his horses. Had given him japonica tablets once or twice. But not for the night. That was the night-sister's job. She went off duty at eight and came on at eight. Retired between ten and eleven. Up at five.

'"A long day, sister?"

'"I think the older one gets, the less sleep one wants. I shall be sixty next month."

'"I'd have put you at much younger than that."

'She smiled.

'"It's the regular life."

'"Sister Helena's younger, I think."

'"Very much younger. She's only thirty-two."

'"I hope to see her," I said, "at three o'clock."

'"I'll see to that. I'm off duty, you see, from two till four."

'"You're very good. In another room per-haps."

'"I think that would be best."

'Then I drove back to the village. The Chief Constable was at the police-station, and he and the superintendent and I had half an hour's talk. Coroner's Inquest on Friday. Well, that's all right. I arranged to see him at five, to suggest the witnesses. The Mother Superior is a by-word. An autocrat, and said to be terribly strict. The staff undoubtedly fear her. So do the tradesmen. If a workman is sent for, the man drops everything else. Her custom's worth having, of course; but it's more than that. I asked if they'd met her. The Chief Constable shook his head. The super-

51

intendent replied, "First time this morning, sir: and I don't want to meet her again. She might have been made of black ice. What d'you propose? she says. I said a man on the terrace and one at the gates. And the door of the room to be locked, an' the House Surgeon keep the key. My lawyer's coming, she says. If you exceed your duty, he'll deal with you. I'll say I was glad to get out."

'The Home has a big reputation in Ne'er-do-well. Said to be very expensive. Big men come down from London to operate. Spare rooms in Paterson's house, so that London doctors and surgeons can stay the night. The sisters never leave the grounds: sometimes seen in the meadows, walking in pairs. The porteress is a tartar – the back-door one. The baker, butcher etc. have to watch their step. Their bills are never questioned, so the Home gets only the best. Plenty of fuel in the winter, though every-one else goes short. Nobody ever knows what patients are there. Some of the staff live out, but they never talk. "She's got them all where they belong, if you ask me."

'Then I got through to London, to say that all was well. I never like saying much on an open line. I had some lunch and dictated a short report. I told them the name of Lord St Amant's Bank – I got that from his cheque-book of course – asked them to get hold of his lawyers and arrange for a clerk to go to his place in Berkshire with one of our men. Curfew Place, not very far from Ascot. That I had got from the Home. And they had his cousin's address, as the next of kin. He's the heir. The Chief Constable's wiring to him.

'At a quarter to three I was back at the Nursing Home. I took Rogers with me and told him to see the head gardener and learn what he could. Are the grounds patrolled at night, and that sort of thing. Then I visited the men at the gates and told them to watch for the Press. "If any reporter gets past you, that's a dereliction of duty – I'll run you myself."

'As I entered the house, Sister Geneviève came out of the porter's lodge. "Will you come this way, Superintendent?" Presently she opened a door on which was the letter C, and I followed her into a chamber which was simple, but not austere. A writing-table, a bowl of flowers and two or three easy chairs. By the window a nun was standing, looking out. As she turned, "Superintendent Falcon – Sister Helena," said Sister Geneviève. Then she withdrew, and we two were left alone.

'We both said "How d'ye do."

'"What beautiful roses," I said. "Your head-gardener must be an expert."

'"He's very good."

'"I rather expect that this is a consulting-room?"

'"Yes, it is one of three.'

'"I shall be a little time, so may we sit down?"

'She took an upright chair and set it with its back to the light. I took my seat on the arm of an easy chair.

'She's a most beautiful girl. Really lovely features and large brown eyes. High breeding stood right out, but her countenance had been refined by the holy life she had led. I've never seen a Madonna that rang so true.

'"Sister Helena, I'm going to be very frank, and I'm sure you'll be frank with me. I'm out of Scotland Yard and I've come to try and find out why Lord St Amant died. It's a very tragic business. He was such a splendid man." Her eyes were upon the ground, but I saw she was breathing fast. "Now I know that you were his night-sister. How many patients were in your charge last night?"

'"Five."

'"All the patients on the terrace but one?"

'"Yes. The patient in Number Three has a nurse to himself."

'"I see. Do the five keep you very busy?"

'"No."

'"Do you wait for them to ring? Or do you look into their rooms, whether they ring or no?"

'"I don't wait for them to ring."

'"You visit them all in turn to see how they're getting on?"

"'Yes."

"'But once they're asleep, you don't?"

"'Sometimes I just look in, to see they're all right."

"'From the terrace perhaps?"

"'Sometimes. In weather like this. Opening a door makes a noise."

"'Supposing you see a light on."

"'I wait. If it isn't put out, I go in."

"'For the last few days, I think, all the windows have stood wide open by day and night."

"'Yes."

"'Have the curtains been drawn?"

"'Only in Number Two and Number Three."

"'Number Three has a special nurse. What about Number Two?"

"'He fears that the morning light may wake him up."

"'Suppose you're visiting someone, and someone else rings for you."

"'Whenever my bell is rung, a small red light comes on in every patient's room. It doesn't disturb the patient, but I see the glow at once."

"'I see. You come on at eight?"

"'Yes."

"'And you visit the five at once?"

"'Yes."

"'To pass the time of day and show that you're there?"

"'Yes.'"

"'Now we come to last night. You visited Lord St Amant soon after eight?'"

"'Yes.'"

"'How did he seem?'"

"'His usual self.'"

"'Cheerful?'"

"'Yes, very cheerful. He always was.'"

"'His temperament was gay?'"

"'Yes.'"

"'Did he call you St Helena?'"

'Her eyes met mine for a moment. Then she nodded her head.

"'When did you see him next?'"

"'Just about ten o'clock. I took him some Ovaltine.'"

"'Was that usual?'"

"'Yes. I always took him a cup about that time.'"

"'And the next time?'"

"'I think about half an hour later. I went to collect the cup.'"

"'Did you bid him goodnight then?'"

"'No. He used to get up after that, to rinse out his mouth.'"

"'I see. So you went back again?'"

"'Yes, in a quarter of an hour.'"

"'What did you do then?'"

"'I put two japonica tablets by his side.'"

"'Did you have any speech with him?'"

"'Yes – for a minute or two.'"

"'He was always ready to talk?'"

"'Yes."

"'Gay as ever?"

"'Yes."

"'Did you finally say goodnight?"

"'Yes."

"'Did you switch off the light?"

"'No. I left that to him."

"'Did you visit him again last night?"

"'No. I just looked into his room, but he was asleep."

"'Are you quite sure he was asleep?"

'She caught her breath. Then–

"'I didn't put on the light, but I thought he was."

"'Perhaps you looked in from the terrace."

"'Yes, I did."

"'But how can you see at all?"

"'I use a torch."

"'I see. And you keep the light on the ground?"

"'Yes."

"'How do you get to the terrace?"

"'Through one of the patient's rooms."

"'I see. And you leave it in the same way?"

"'Yes."

"'Usually One and Six?"

"'No. Number Two sleeps very sound, so I usually pass through his room."

"'What time was it, when you just looked into his room?"

"'It was just about three."

"'How d'you remember that?"

57

'"Because I always go round at about that time."

'"I quite understand. Now tell me this, Sister Helena. During last night, did you hear or see anything unusual either upon the terrace or in the house?"

'"No."

'"No light in the meadows?"

'"No."

'"I want you to think for a moment. Think of the hours between eleven and six... Did anything at all occur during those seven hours that seemed irregular?"

'She sat for a moment, thinking. Then–

'"Nothing," she said.

'"You went to call Lord St Amant at six o'clock?"

'"I think it was a few minutes past."

'"You took in his tea."

'"Yes."

'"What did you find?"

'Her head went down.

'"I found him dead."

'"You had no doubt?"

'"Oh, no."

'"There was no mistaking it?"

'She shook her head.

'"His eyes were open?"

'"Yes."

'"Please tell me the impression you got."

'"He looked ... as if ... he'd been taken by surprise."

'She burst into tears there, and I waited for three or four minutes, until she was more composed.

'"I'm sorry," she said at last. "But it was such a dreadful moment."

'"It must have been. I'm – terribly sorry for you."

'She raised her head at that, and looked me full in the eyes.

'"It's a sister's duty," she said, "to deal with life and death."

'"Of course. But sisters are human. The bride of Christ can't put off her womanhood."

'"By which you mean?"

'"That women like you are tender. When they see such a man so dead, it touches their heart. I mean, it touched mine; and I am a policeman, accustomed to violent death."

'She caught her breath. Then–

'"Please go on," she said.

'"What did you do, Sister Helena?"

'"I ran to my pantry and rang both emergency bells."

'"Whom do they summon?"

'"The Mother Superior and the House Surgeon."

'"Yes."

'"Then I called another sister and we waited by the door of the room."

'"Did she go in?"

'"For a moment – yes."

'"Alone?"

'"I watched from the door. She brought me out a chair, so that I could sit down."

'"And then?"

'"We waited outside the room. Then the Mother Superior arrived and I told her Lord St Amant was dead."

'"Did she go in?"

'"Yes."

'"Alone?"

'"No, I went in with her and stood by the door."

'"Was anything touched?"

'"I don't think so."

'"Were the tablets still in the spoon?"

'"No."

'"And then?"

'"The Mother Superior asked what I had to say: and I told her that I had known nothing until I came into the room."

'"And then?"

'"The House Surgeon arrived."

'"And then?"

'"He – he made an examination, and I – I began to feel faint. So a sister took me out and I sat on the terrace steps."

'"Were the tablets mentioned?"

'"Yes. He asked me what they were and I said japonica. He asked how many, and I said only two."

'"You were back in the room then?"

'"Yes. They sent for me."

"'Yes.'

"'Then the Mother Superior dismissed us. She sent me back to my quarters and told the other sister to send Sister Geneviève.'

"'But she and the doctor remained?'

"'Yes.'

"'Did you stay in your quarters till now?'

"'Yes.'

"'Did anyone visit you?'

"'The house surgeon came and gave me something to drink.'

"'Did you have a talk?'

"'Yes, he was very kind.'

"'Did he tell you there might be an Inquest?'

"'Yes.'

"'Anything else?'

"'He asked if at any time I had had any reason to think that Lord St Amant was not in excellent health.'

"'What did you say?'

"'None.'

"'Did anyone else visit you?'

"'The Mother Superior.'

"'What did she say?'

"'I don't think I have the right to repeat what she said.'

"'In the ordinary way, no. But I'll leave it there for the moment. I may have to ask you again.'

"'What d'you mean – in the ordinary way?'

"'It may be found that his lordship died an

unnatural death."

'"You think he did?"

'I looked at her very straight.

'"D'you think that his death was natural?"

'After a little, she spoke in a very low voice.

'"Why don't you think so?"

'"Well, he was so well – and then ... that – that terrible look on his face."

'She put her face in her hands and began to weep again.

'"To give her time, I went to the writing-table, took a sheet of paper and made some notes.

'Suddenly she burst out.

'"But who would want to kill him? He was so charming and gentle in every way."

'I turned on my chair.

'"That's what I've got to find out – if anyone did. Before very long I shall know whether or no he was killed. And if he was and if I'm to find out who did it, I must have everyone's help. You see, Sister Helena, I haven't got second sight. I've just been questioning you: and I'm sure you've told me the truth. But it may very well be that you have a vital answer to some question I haven't asked. If that is so, please don't hold out on me. And please remember this – that you may not think it is vital, although it is."

'"I see. I'll bear that in mind."

'"Thank you."

'"Will they want me to go to the Inquest?"

'"Yes, I'm afraid they will. But I shall be there and I'll do my best for you."

'"When will it be?"

'"On Friday. I shall take your statement tomorrow, and the Coroner will question you from that."

'"Will he … ask me anything else?"

'"I don't quite see why he should."

'She hesitated. Then–

'"You see, Superintendent, we all have other names. I'm Sister Helena now, but I … used to be somebody else."

'"I know. I'll do my very best to see that you're not asked that. But…"

'"But what?"

'"As things are or may be, I think that I ought to know. But you may depend upon me to tell no one else."

'She told me her name. I hope she didn't see that it shook me, because it did. Her face had been vaguely familiar right from the first; but when she told me her name, I remembered who she was.

'I thanked her and got to my feet.

'"I hope you've been taken off duty."

'"For tonight – yes."

'"I'd like to see you tomorrow. Would midday be all right?"

'"As – as far as I'm concerned."

'"Good. And please don't worry. It's going to be quite all right."

'"It can never be that," she said quietly.

"Not if murder was done."

"'I feel the same," I said. "A masterpiece has been broken. And we have so few today."

"'That's perfectly true."

'As I opened the door for her—

"'You've been very kind," she said.

'And then she was gone.

'I went back to the station then and dictated a further report. Then I drafted her statement and gave it to Roan to type out. Then I went to the mortuary. The surgeons were waiting for me, with certain sealed jars. They handed these to Rogers, who signed a receipt.

"'Anything new?" I asked.

"'A first-class life."

'When Paterson left, I walked with him to his car. I told him I'd seen the night-sister.

"'Was the Mother Superior tiresome?"

"'She wasn't there."

"'You never saw her alone?"

"'Yes."

"'God in heaven," he said. And then, "There'll be a row about that."

"'The day-sister arranged it at my request."

'He nodded.

"'Sister Geneviève is the salt of the earth."

"'You'll be called, of course. I'll bring a draft statement tomorrow, for you to approve."

"'All right."

"'At about eleven o'clock?"

'"Just ask for me."

'Then I saw the Coroner.

'I think he'll be quite all right. I mean, he won't run out. In fact, he himself declared that the Convent must be considered in every possible way. I imagine the Mother Superior has to be thanked for that. Her writ runs everywhere. I suggested whom he should call and said he should have their statements tomorrow afternoon. I then broached the question of revealing the sisters' true names.

'"I hope you'll agree," I said, "that that should not be done. By such revelations, Justice will in no way be served. Only the press will profit: and the Sisters will suffer incredible misery. I mean, all this publicity's bad enough."

'Mercifully, he agreed at once.

'Then we had a short talk. I said that the local superintendent would ask for an adjournment for a week.

'"Do you expect developments?"

'"Yes."

'"You suspect that Lord St Amant was murdered?"

'"I do indeed."

'"Any luck so far?"

'"None."

'"Oh, well," he said. "If I can help, you've only to let me know."

'I thanked him and took my leave.

'Then I saw the Press. They were waiting

in force. "Where the carcase is," you know.

'I told them the bare facts. That St Amant who was perfectly well had suddenly died. That there seemed to be no explanation of how or why he had died. That before we did anything else, we had to find that out. I said I had been sent down because, if he died by design, it was of the utmost importance that experts should be on the spot as soon as possible.

'"Do you suspect foul play?"

'"You mustn't say that. You may say that, in view of all the circumstances, the police have yet to be satisfied that Lord St Amant died a natural death."

'I gave them a lot of details – that's what they like. In fact, I did them well. And then I spoke out.

'"I'll see you like this, whenever I have some news which I think you may well report. But only on this condition – that no reporter enters the Convent grounds. If that occurs, you'll get no more from me. The nursing home is run by a deeply religious House. The sisters are nuns, and their life is very sheltered and very retired. It follows that the publicity which this tragedy must receive is to them a most bitter blow. I'm very sorry for them, and I'm going to do my best to spare them all I can. I hope that you'll do the same. You've got to tell your stories, of course: and you'll do that as you think best. But don't forget that the sisters are holy women, vowed to the service of God, that they work very hard indeed for nothing at all, that this disaster has caused them the very greatest distress. If you can lighten their burden, I'm sure that you will."

'They took it very well – they're a decent crowd.

'Then one of them asked the question I wanted asked.

'"Will any sisters be called?"

'"I think that's possible. If they are, I can't prevent your taking photographs of them. But if you do, you'll make them very unhappy. I hope you'll bear that in mind."

'Then I looked in at the station and called it a day.'

'Poor Superintendent,' said Jenny, 'you must be so terribly tired.'

'No, Mrs Chandos, I've had more tiring days. And being with you three here is the greatest relief. Any comments, Colonel Mansel?'

'I think you've done awfully well.'

'You have, indeed,' said I.

'In fact,' said Jenny, rising, 'we're going to drink your health. Would you like a brandy and soda?'

'I'd rather have a soft drink.'

'We always drink barley-water.'

'Please give me some.'

Mansel spoke.

'He was poisoned, of course. The japonica tablets were taken and two poisoned tablets were left. That could only have been done by someone who knew quite a lot: knew that he had two tablets put by his side and knew that he used to take them during the night. One naturally looks very hard at the occupants of the Home – the sisters, the house-surgeon and the other patients. But the deed might well have been done by a complete outsider.'

'I entirely agree,' said Falcon. 'Access was easy. Deserted meadows, ringed by a very low wall, the terrace in darkness, and French windows wide open all night long. By the way, Mr Chandos, have you a binocular?'

'I have. Would you like to borrow it?'

'If I may. I want to see how much I can see from the road.'

'Bell shall give it to you before you go off. It's very powerful.'

'Good. Casual observation might have been kept from a car. As for special, close observation – well, the meadows and the terrace by night would offer a perfect field. I mean, you could hardly go wrong.'

'Who,' said Mansel, 'who knew he was in the Home and where he was likely to be put?'

'Ah,' said Falcon. 'To find the answer to that may be very hard.'

There was a little silence. Then– 'I feel,' said I, 'that a woman committed the crime.'

'Why d'you say that, Mr Chandos?'

68

'I don't think a man would have thrown away the tablet you found.'

'It may have been dropped.'

'I don't think a man would have dropped it. The man who would do such a thing would have been more careful than that.'

'What would you have done with it – them?'

'Swallowed them,' said I.

'So should I,' said Falcon. 'But then we're rather good at covering up. Never mind. A man has pockets, but a woman has not. In any event, I'm inclined to agree with you. It looks to me much more like a woman's crime.'

'You've a friend in the day-nurse,' said Mansel.

'I think I have. Had I had to question Sister Helena in the presence of the Mother Superior, to a great extent I should have gone empty away. And it would have been a dreadful ordeal for us both. From what Paterson said, I'm afraid Sister Geneviève will be roasted for what she did.'

'A courageous woman,' said Mansel. 'But I don't think you'll see the Madonna alone again.'

'Nor do I. But that won't matter so much. At least, I hope it won't.'

'Now what have you got, Falcon?'

'The tablet and Dallas' contribution. That may or may not be of value. But that is all.'

'Not bad for the very first day.'

'No, I've been very lucky.'

'Acquaintances?'

'London is on that now. His papers may reveal something. The Will may be a pointer – you never know. Who stood to gain by his death?'

'I don't like that one,' said Mansel.

'Neither do I. But there must be a motive somewhere.'

'Somehow I don't think it was gain. Jealousy, yes. Hatred. But somehow not gain.'

'I'm inclined to agree; but I can't rule anything out. There are three more patients on the terrace. I can hardly believe that one of them is concerned, but I'll have to see them tomorrow.'

'Dallas sounds rather glib.'

'I'm with you there. I'm not quite sure of the man. But Paterson says that he can't put his foot to the ground.'

'And after the Inquest?'

'I shall go to Curfew Place. His servants may be able to help.'

'House-surgeon all right?' said I.

'I think so. He's rather hard to sum up. But then at this stage I can take no one on trust.'

'Except the night-sister,' said Jenny.

'Quite right, Mrs Chandos. She is above suspicion. So are they all, more or less. But as for her – well, I might as well suspect you.'

There was a little silence. Then–

'Superintendent,' said Jenny, 'may I ask you a personal question?'

'Of course.'

'Well, this evening you've told us exactly not only what you have done, but what you have seen and heard. And very much more than that. You have repeated in detail each conversation you've had. Question and answer, over and over again. How on earth can you remember?'

Falcon smiled.

'It's a matter of practice, Mrs Chandos. If you'd practised as long as I have, you would be able to do exactly the same. You see, very early on I realized this – that I should never get on terms with a witness, if he saw that what he was saying was being taken down. Not the terms I wanted to be on. Yet sometimes every word – almost every inflection – might have an important bearing upon the case. And so I began to train my memory – make it into a record, like that of a dictaphone. I've played it to you this evening. After thirty years it's getting quite good.'

'I think it's marvellous.'

'So it is,' said Mansel. 'I need hardly add that, for obvious reasons, such a faculty is quite invaluable.'

'I've found it so,' said Falcon, 'again and again. Of course the impression fades. But if it's important, I dictate it while it is clear.'

What more was said, I forget: but very

soon after that, we all of us went to bed.

Not till the Inquest was over did Falcon go on with his tale; for on the following night he spent an hour or more in the curtilage of the Home. It was past eleven o'clock by the time he got back, and, though he was ready to talk, Jenny would not let him, but put on some Chopin records, to stop our mouths. So, after a quiet half hour, we all retired. But on Friday, the following evening, Falcon sat back in his chair and told us the truth.

'Yesterday morning I took the road past the Home. I stopped by the side of the way and used your binocular. I could see right into the rooms. I saw a sister moving in Dallas' room. But I couldn't see any detail. If close observation was kept, it was kept in the meadows by night.

'Then I went to the station and had a word with the Yard. Inspector Welcome is down at Curfew Place. The solicitors are most helpful. They're the executors, too, and Welcome's been given a room and all facilities. The new Lord St Amant, a cousin, is overseas. The tablet I found disclosed no fingermarks, but was japonica. The analysis was being done.

'Then I set Rogers to work – to see if any car had been noticed at rest not far from the Home on Monday or Tuesday night. And then I left for the Home, taking the statements with me.'

'Sister Helena's and the House-Surgeon's?'

'That's right. For them to approve.

'When I arrived, the porteress asked me to wait. After a minute or two, a sister appeared and asked me to come with her. I knew what that meant.

'The Mother Superior received me alone.

'She was seated at her table, but she didn't rise and she didn't ask me to sit down. She neither moved nor spoke. I felt that something must be done. Accordingly, I sat down and looked at my watch. Then–

'"Madam,' I said, "I assume that you wish to see me. I beg that you'll tell me why, for I have a great deal to do. I hope you have some information which you think that I ought to know."

'"I wished to see you," she said, "to tell you this – that I will permit no sister of mine to be questioned without my consent."

'"In that case I must ask your consent to see Sister Helena at twelve o'clock. And Sister Geneviève: but not at that hour."

'"I am engaged at twelve. Tomorrow perhaps."

'"I'm afraid I must see her this morning. I have the draft of her statement, for her to revise."

'"Give it to me."

'"That would be most improper. I have no objection to your being present, when I go through it with her."

'"*No objection?*"

'The words flamed.

'"None," said I. "But I must do it this morning, because the Coroner must have it this afternoon. The Inquest will be held tomorrow at two o'clock. I formally ask you to allow Sister Helena to attend."

'"And if I refuse?"

'"Madam," said I, "a summons to attend will be served upon her today. If she fails to obey it – well, I can't answer to the coroner, but I know what the Press will do."

'"What will they do?"

'"Report it in banner headlines."

'There was a little silence. Pride was fighting with Discretion – a battle royal. At length–

'"If I must–"

'I got to my feet.

'"Madam, there must be no 'if'. Church and State – both are subject to the Law. I am a Superintendent of the CID: but if I exceed a speed-limit, I can be summoned and fined. I am ready to show you the greatest regard; but if that conflicts with my duty, my duty will take precedence of my regard. At your convenience, I'm going to question you."

'"*Me?*"

'"On the rules and habits and customs of this establishment. If you embarrass me, I shall have to report the fact to my superiors.

74

They have sent me here, to get to the bottom of this most grievous affair. The Home Office is behind them in all they do."

'"What do you want?"

'"I want you to tell your people – sisters and staff – that they must speak freely to me or my men, must give us every assistance, volunteer information they think that we ought to have. If I have any difficulty, Madam, I want to be able to come to you, lay the matter before you and ask your help and advice. I want to hear your suggestions and what you think. I want to be on those terms with the lady whose word is law within these walls."

'There was a long silence. Then–

'"Come back at twelve," she said. "Sister Helena will be here."

'Good for you,' cried Mansel, and Jenny was clapping her hands.

'It's an old trick,' said Falcon, 'that I learned in the First Great War. I had a rogue in my troop, so I gave him a stripe. He made the best lance-corporal I've ever seen.

'I took my leave of her and ran into Paterson. He was then too busy to talk, but said I could see two patients out of the three. The third was too ill and had been for more than a week. So I saw the two.'

'Two out of the three?' said Jenny.

'My fault, Mrs Chandos. It's an important point, and I ought to have made it clear. Six rooms on the terrace. Number Four was St Amant's room. Dallas is Number Five. The patient in Number Three is dying hard – under morphia most of the time. The patient in Number One is seriously ill – too ill to be interviewed. As I'd seen Dallas, Two and Six were left.

'Number Two, I wrote off at once. He was very old and shaky. Had been in the Indian Civil for most of his life. He'd known St Amant's father and talked about nothing else. Had no idea that St Amant was two rooms off. "If only they'd told me, I would have sent in my card. I hope he didn't know I was here. You see, when I was in Lahore…" I gave up as soon as I could, and visited Number Six.

'Number Six made me think. His name is Berryman – aged, he said, thirty-one. When Paterson had left us–

'"Head Sleuth?" he said, with a lazy look in his eyes.

'"Some people might call me that."

'"A gentleman copper. Hence the promotion, of course."

'"That's not for me to say."

'"Winchester?"

'"No. And my antecedents don't matter. What does matter is that Lord St Amant is dead."

'"D'you know what I'd do to the fellow that bumped him off?"

"'What?' said I.

"'Give him a drink.'

"'Would you now?' said I, and took a chair.

"'One lord the less. You see, I'm what you'd call Labour.'

"'I see. But you prefer this Home to a casual ward.'

"'I had no say in the matter. My – my relatives sent me here.'

"'I see. When did you learn that Lord St Amant was dead?'

'He pointed to a paper, lying on the foot of his bed.

"'Not till this morning?'

"'No. I knew there was something afoot.'

"'How did you know that?'

"'Because The Virgin Goddess failed to appear.'

"'I see.'

"'*Alias* Lady Rosemary Vernon.'

"'Indeed?' said I, masking annoyance with surprise.

"'And you call yourself a sleuth.'

"'I don't, as a matter of fact: but that's neither here nor there. Whoever Sister Helena is is nothing to do with me. And now let's get back on the rails. It was her failure to call you that told you that something was wrong.'

"'Then one of your bluebottles showed himself on the terrace.'

"'Didn't you ask what that meant?'

"'Geneviève wouldn't talk: and Paterson

77

was what is called uncommunicative."

"'Why did you say that Lord St Amant had been bumped off?'"

"'Be your age.'"

"'I want to know, please.'"

"'Well, I assumed he had. You're not down here for nothing.'" He pointed to the paper. 'Head Sleuths make headlines.'

"'I see. Did you know Lord St Amant was here?'"

"'How should I?'"

"'Does that mean that you didn't?'"

"'I didn't know he was here.'"

"'He died on Tuesday night. Cast your mind back for a moment. Did you sleep right through that night? Or were you awake at all?'"

"'I woke up now and again.'"

"'Pain?'"

"'Yes, damn you. Pain.'"

"'I'm sorry for that. What do you do for it?'"

"'What can I do, but bear it?'"

"'If it was bad, I think I should ring for the sister and ask for some dope.'"

"'I do sometimes.'"

"'Anyway, on Tuesday night, you woke up more than once.'"

"'Correct.'"

"'Did anything wake you up except the pain?'"

"'I don't understand.'"

"'Did anything else rouse you? Did you

78

ever wake up to find that you had no pain?"

'"I don't think so."

'"Did you hear any sound that night, for which you couldn't account?"

'"Not that I can remember."

'"Did you see anything unusual? Some light, for instance, that you had not seen before?"

Berryman shook his head.

'"I see you've a torch by your side. What do you use that for?"

'"If I want a drink, it saves switching on the light."

'"I see." I got to my feet. "Well, now I must go."

'"See you again?"

'"Perhaps."

'"Any progress to report?"

'"Perhaps."

'"But not to me?"

'"No."

'I left his room for the terrace and passed to the parapet. I stood still there for a moment, looking at the meadows and considering Berryman. That I had no use for him, is beside the point. A most unpleasant type. But I was perfectly sure that he was covering up. More. His studied truculence showed that he was afraid. For some absurd reason, I resented his recognition of Lady Rosemary Vernon. But his casual disclosure of her private name had made me more angry than

79

a policeman should ever get.'

'By God, I don't blame you,' I said.

'Well, when I'd calmed down, I ventured to put my head into Dallas' room.

'"At last. Good morning, Superintendent. I'm happy to say that I have some news for you."

'"Your memory has responded?"

'"It has, indeed. Strangely enough, I remembered when first I woke up last night."

'I nodded.

'"When you come to think," I said, "that was the likeliest moment for such a thing to occur."

'"Of course. The witching hour. We ought to have thought of that."

'"I'm glad we didn't. When memory is contrary, it's best to leave her alone."

'"What a lot lies in gender! Of course, you're perfectly right. Ignore the capricious jade, and she comes to heel."

'"I've found that so."

'"What a man you are!"

'"Why d'you say that?" said I.

'"Because you haven't yet asked me what it was that I heard or saw at precisely a quarter to two in the morning of yesterday."

'"I don't want to rush you," I said. "I know you'll tell me all right."

'"Your restraint is remarkable. That's why you're where you are. Never mind. I now remember that I saw the flash of a torch."

"'No doubt at all?'"

"'None. I saw it upon the terrace. Only a flash. Put your head close to my pillows.' I did as he said. "Now, looking out of those windows, what do you see?'"

"'I see the turn of the parapet, just where it reaches the steps.'"

"'That was where the light fell. But only for an instant of time. Whether the torch was switched off or the beam was diverted, of course I can't possibly say. But the flash was there.'"

"'It wasn't the light from some room?'"

"'Oh, no. That would have been diffused. This was limited and concentrated. It was the light of a torch.'"

"'I quite understand. And now let me hand something back. What a witness you'd make!'"

"'If you possibly can, please preserve the conditional mood.'"

'I laughed.

"'You won't be called tomorrow. I can't say more than that – except, Mr Dallas, that I am greatly obliged. Please keep this to yourself.'"

"'Depend upon that, Superintendent. May I ask how you're getting on?'"

'I shrugged my shoulders.

"'Routine stuff, for the moment. No more than that.'"

"'Have you seen any other patients?'"

"'Yes, I've just visited two.'"

"'Have you made the acquaintance of Mr Berryman?'"

"'Yes,' I said. 'How did you know he was here?'"

"'St Amant told me that.'"

"'How did he know?'"

"'He saw him from the terrace, before I called him. St Amant was laughing about it.'"

"'Why?'"

"'Apparently Berryman's one of these Eton and Labour lads. Urges the dockers to strike, and then goes home to bed in Grosvenor Square. His father and St Amant's were lifelong friends, and when Berryman went to Eton, St Amant was asked to keep an eye on him. In fact, for a while, he was St Amant's fag. 'I'm afraid,' he said, 'he doesn't do me much credit.' 'I hope you thrashed him,' I said. 'I had to once or twice. Not for his failings as a fag, but for breaches of discipline. He had to be fired in the end. And he's gone on as he began. Conscientious Objector in the War, and stoking the fires of class-hatred right and left. In view of the speeches he makes, it's rather amusing to find such a fellow here.' 'I hope,' I said, 'I hope he's confined to his room.' 'I hope so, too,' said St Amant, thoughtfully.'"

"'An unpleasant type,' I said. 'I must confess he didn't appeal to me.'"

"'The king of cads,' said Dallas. 'I don't mind honest Labour. For a man like John

Burns, I have an immense respect. But I cannot stand these bastards. You're sure he's confined to bed? I don't want him walking in here."

"'I've no idea," I said. "But I'm sure you could deal with him."

"'Perhaps. But I have reached an age, Superintendent, at which friction of any kind has become repugnant to me. It was not always so. I used to enjoy a really sharp dispute. Let us say that my rapier was loose. But now, at sixty-two, I'm much more peaceable. I hope Dracona is not a thorn in your side."

"'Oh, no," said I. "She doesn't like it, of course: but I think she understands that I'm out to help."

"'What a man!" said Dallas. "Dracona eats out of his hand."

"'I never said that," said I.

"'I know, I know. Miracles are in your line. You're heading for canonization. If you go on like this, you'll become St Falcon of Ne'er-do-well. Pilgrims will repair in great numbers to Scotland Yard. By the way, have you seen your star turn?"

"'Yes, I have."

"'Isn't she a winner? All wrong for her to be here. Born to be a chatelaine – the mistress of a proud duchy, the mother of glorious sons. The veil, you know, has much to answer for."

'As I got to my feet–

'"I'm afraid," I said, "there's something in what you say."

'"But what a man!" said Dallas.

'We, both of us, laughed at that, and I took my leave.

'I saw a sister and asked where the House Surgeon was. She asked me to wait, and, after three or four minutes, Paterson came. By my desire we sought a consulting room.

'"Here's your draft statement," I said. "Will you look it through and make what corrections you please?"

'"For the Coroner?"

'"Yes."

'He read it through, made a revision or two, put in his Christian names and gave it back.

'Then—

'"There's been," he said, "the devil and all to pay."

'"Because I saw Sister Helena?"

'"Yes."

'"I gathered that. I hope I've straightened things out."

'He looked at me very hard.

'"Well, I hope you have," he said: "for life's quite wearing enough in the ordinary way. I mean, if ever there was one, she is a martinet. She's a very good woman, you know. She'd go to the stake for one of her principles, and though you might not think it, she loves her flock. And she runs this Home, as could no man or woman I've ever met.

Her efficiency is staggering. But talk about being stiff-necked… Of course she was born out of time. She ought to have been an abbess – and more than that."

"'We've had a straight talk," I said. "And I hope very much that now she will see the wisdom of putting some trust in me."

"'Very good indeed. And how d'you like Berryman?"

"'I don't like him very much. I shouldn't think anyone does."

"'Between you and me, Superintendent, the man is a poisonous cad."

"'Why d'you say that?"

"'He's been fit to walk for a week – and the lavatory's fifty feet off. On Monday last I found he was still using a bed-pan. What about that?"

"'That," said I, "is atrocious."

"'To degrade these wonderful women in that disgusting way!"

"'And all the time he can walk?"

"'Perfectly well. But he's too damned lazy to move. I ordered him to bathe on Sunday and saw him to the bathroom myself. I don't think he's had a bath since."

"'Can't you get rid of him?"

"'He's leaving on Saturday. In my opinion, he's quite fit enough to go now."

"'I asked him how he was sleeping: he said that the pain woke him from time to time."

"'It may, but it's not severe. And he has his

tablets there. And if he wants any more, he's only to ring."

'"I see. You give japonica freely?"

'"Yes. It's completely harmless and seems to work very well. No news of the analysis yet?"

'I shook my head.

'"I'll tell you as soon as I hear."

'We parted then: and as it was twenty to twelve, I made my way to the meadows and strolled there for a quarter of an hour. As you will agree, I had plenty of food for thought.

'That Berryman had seen St Amant, I had no doubt. What do you say, Colonel Mansel?'

'I think he must have,' said Mansel. 'St Amant was on the terrace, while he was within his room. Now by day the man without is always more apparent to the man within than is the man within to the man without. Yet St Amant recognized him. And if anyone passes your window, you always look up.'

'I agree. So Berryman lied when he said that he didn't know that St Amant was there. Then he omitted to tell me that he had known St Amant all his life. I don't think that's putting it too high.'

'Certainly not,' said I. 'They'd been at school together, and their fathers were lifelong friends. They must have met sometimes, for St Amant expressed the hope that he wouldn't come into his room.'

'Exactly. Then he concealed the fact that,

as in St Amant's case, tablets were put by his side. Then he possesses a torch. I don't attach a great deal of importance to that, for he must have expected me, and it would have been so easy to put it away. Still, I didn't think much of his reason for keeping it there. For the switch was to hand. And Dallas saw the flash of a torch. Then – the man can walk. He walked to the bathroom on Sunday. Finally, he had no cause to love the man who is dead.'

'As like as not,' said Mansel, 'he hated his guts.'

'I think it probable. But I don't want to put it too high. The thrashings may well have rankled, and there may have been other things. Besides, the howling cad dislikes the gentleman. That doesn't mean that he wants to bump him off. But that sort of feeling sometimes runs very high.'

Jenny lifted her voice.

'I don't wonder he was afraid when you came into his room.'

Falcon smiled.

'Nor do I, Mrs Chandos. But that is not evidence of guilt. Many an innocent man has been frightened to death, because, if the truth were known, things would look very black for him. But of course fear makes you think. And I don't mind admitting to you that I'm looking at him very hard. So hard that, when he leaves, Mr Berryman will be watched. I don't want him to leave the country before I can see him again.

'At precisely twelve o'clock I knocked on the door of the Mother Superior's room. Sister Helena opened the door and ushered me in. I bowed to them both. Then I produced the statement.

'"With your permission, Madam, Sister Helena will read this through and say if there is anything in it to which she cannot subscribe. If there is, it will be altered at once. And then, if you please, I should like you to read it yourself."

'"Very well."

'There were one or two slight corrections, but nothing of any account. When these had been made, I gave it to the Mother Superior. She perused it with a slight frown. Then she addressed Sister Helena. 'When you looked in at three o'clock, you saw nothing amiss?' 'Nothing, *ma mère*.' Then she addressed herself to me.

'"You will understand, Superintendent, that Lord St Amant was never seriously ill. The sister was, therefore, more concerned not to rouse him than she was to observe his condition. Had he been seriously ill, the reverse would have been the case."

'"I quite understand, Madam."

'She handed the statement back.

'"Have you any more questions to put to Sister Helena?"

88

""A few, if you please."

""Very well."

""Tell me, Sister Helena, have you any tablets at all, except japonica?"

""No. When we had tried japonica, the others were all withdrawn."

""You use japonica at your discretion."

""Not altogether. I'm allowed to give two or three, as I see fit. But not more than three in two hours."

""Did you give them to other patients?"

""Oh, yes."

""Who did you give them to?"

""Mr Dallas and Mr Berryman. Both have pain."

""Do you wait for them to ask?"

""No. I always put two by their side, when I say goodnight. If they want any more in the night, they let me know."

""You place them in the bowl of a spoon?"

""Yes."

""What about injections?"

""I only give them by order."

""Had any been ordered that night?"

""No."

""Have you *ampoules* at your disposal?"

""Only penicillin. That is kept in the refrigerator."

""Did you look into all the rooms about three o'clock?"

""Yes."

""Did you go into any room?"

"'I passed through Sir Arthur Brake's – that's Number Two."

"'I take it that he's the patient that sleeps so sound."

"'Yes."

"'Did you go into any other?"

"'Only Number One. That's Admiral Lacey's room."

"'I understand that he's very ill."

"'Yes. That was why I went in."

"'To have, shall we say, a close-up?"

"'Yes."

"'What about Number Three?"

"'He's being specially nursed. I just showed myself to the Sister, in case she wanted me."

"'Not counting Number Two, through which you passed, you only went into one?"

"'Yes."

"'So far as you could see, were the other patients asleep?"

"'Yes."

"'How long did that round take you on Tuesday night?"

"'I should say about a quarter of an hour."

"'Did you start at three o'clock?"

"'No. About five minutes to."

"'Thank you."

'I looked at the Mother Superior.

"'The Inquest, madam, will be held to-morrow at two o'clock. I shall not be called, but I shall be there. Entirely between us three, I have seen the Coroner and he has expressed his intention of showing the utmost consideration to any Sister called. I have also seen the Press, and I've done my best with them. I have some influence there, because they find it pays to keep in with me. If they do as I ask, I'm more inclined to talk.

"'I should like to call for Sister Helena at half past one. I expect both you and she would like another Sister to go with her. I'm going to try to arrange to bring them into the court by a private way."

"'Thank you," said the Mother Superior. "The two will be ready and waiting to-morrow at half past one. Have you any more questions to ask Sister Helena?"

"'No more questions for the moment, but I have a request to make"

"'Yes."

"'Madam, the thing is this. On the table beside the bed were a glass and a spoon. These are being tested for fingerprints. Two sets of prints will, I imagine, be found – on the glass at any rate. One will be those of Sister Helena. But I cannot be sure that they are her fingerprints, unless she allows me to take an impression of hers. And I must know whose they are.

"'If she will allow me to take it, the moment the prints have been checked she shall have the impression back."

'The Mother Superior turned to Sister Helena.

'"Have you any objection?"

'"None at all, *ma mère.*"

'The Mother Superior returned to me.

'"Can you take them here, Superintendent?"

'"At once, if you please."

'It was done in a minute, of course: but I did hate doing it so to Sister Helena. We very often obtain them by means of a trick. But I couldn't treat her like that. I had to ask straight out.

'When it was over—

'"Thank you very much," I said.

'"Anything else, Superintendent?"

'"No, madam."

'"Very well. You may leave us, Sister Helena."

'I opened the door, and the Sister bowed and withdrew.

'As I closed it behind her—

'"I understand, Superintendent, that you have been told the name which Sister Helena used to bear."

'"I have, madam. That was something which it was right I should know."

'"It must not be divulged in Court."

'"It will not be divulged, madam."

'"Is that your doing?"

'"Yes."

'"What about photographs?"

'"I've done my utmost, madam. I hope that none will be taken. I daren't put it higher than that."

'"Very well. Is there anything else?"

'"By your leave, madam, I should like to see the night-sister of Number Three."

'"Why do you wish to see her?"

'"Because she was on duty all night in the room which is next to the room in which Lord St Amant died."

'"Four sisters share the duty in this particular case. Of course they do other work: but six hours on end in that room is long enough. One comes on at eight in the morning, another at two: another at eight in the evening and another again at two."

'"I should like to see the two who are on duty at night."

'"Very well. The first of the two shall be here at three o'clock."

'"If you please, madam."'

Falcon looked from Mansel to me. Then—

'I don't have to tell you,' he said, 'that I should much have preferred to see them alone. The atmosphere created by the Mother Superior's presence is as forbidding as it is invulnerable. Still, my relations with her had so much improved that it would have been sheer folly to raise such a delicate point.'

'I agree,' said Mansel. 'You'd've lost more ground than you'd made. But it is most unfortunate. I don't suggest that the questions you ask in her presence are ever answered with lies: but the fear of incurring her displeasure by something they say is bound, I think, to command every answer you get.'

'As you will see,' said Falcon.

'I drove back to the station then, saw the Chief Constable and dictated a report to the Yard. In this I said that, if nothing broke down here, I proposed to return on Saturday, make a report in person and then go to Curfew Place. Rogers, of course, will remain at Ne'er-do-well. I plan to be back on Tuesday or Wednesday evening. May I come here, Mrs Chandos?'

'Your room will be waiting,' said Jenny.

'You're sure that you've no other guests that–'

'We haven't, indeed. We live very quietly now.'

'You're very good to me.'

'Please don't say that, Superintendent. We're only so sorry you have to be out all day.'

'Mrs Chandos,' said Mansel, 'always means what she says. As for your host and myself we count it a very great privilege to be admitted to your counsel.'

'That's less than the truth,' said I. 'But I know that I speak for us both, when I say that, because you've begun, there is no reason at all why you should go on. And we don't want you to get tired.'

'Mr Chandos,' said Falcon, 'I think I'm

right in saying that you never worked alone. If you had, you would know what a blessed relief it is to be able to talk. Rogers is very good; but I cannot talk to him as I can talk to you. Add to that that I look for your reactions to what I say. In a case like this, his would be – I won't say valueless, because that wouldn't be fair: but of very much less account. Neither you nor Colonel Mansel could do Rogers' job. He knows what to look for, and in his particular line he's a tower of strength. But ordinary, routine work is not going to help us here. In this deep and delicate case, outlook, habits and manners make up the bottle of hay in which the needle called motive is lying concealed.

'And now let me take up my tale.

'I lunched with Rogers. Then we went to his room and I heard what he had to say. Only one thing of importance. A car was seen by a cyclist on Monday night. About eleven o'clock. A handsome, pale-grey saloon. It was berthed just off the road, and its lights were out. Rogers was shown the place. It took him seven minutes to walk from there to the Home. Monday, of course – not Tuesday. But, as I have pointed out, if the crime was done by a stranger, a reconnaissance had to be made. The gardeners were not very helpful. In view of my talk with the Mother Superior, I told him to try them again. Oh, by the way, no marks at all on the wall. But this is very easy to scale.

'Then I went back to the station and read and signed my report. Whilst I was there, a note from the Yard came in. Sir William was doing the analysis – at least, it was in his hands. They hoped to have the result by Friday midday. St Amant's prints on everything but the spoon. Somebody else's prints on the spoon and the glass. A hundred to one they're those of Sister Helena.

'Then I drove back to the Home.

'The first of the special night-nurses for Number Three is called Sister Josephine. She has a very sweet face, but it's easy enough to see why she took the veil. She did it to obtain sanctuary. Very earnest, very shy, and next to no brain. Utterly and completely helpless, and only too thankful not to have to think for herself.

'The Mother Superior introduced us and the poor girl looked ready to sink into the ground. I endeavoured to reassure her as best I could.

'"When I first came here, Sister Josephine, I felt very strange and I don't mind confessing to you that I wished that somebody else had been sent in my stead. But everyone here has been so kind and understanding that I don't feel a stranger now. For all that, I've still got a lot to learn, and the only way I can learn it is by asking questions. So now I'm going to ask some of you.

"'I think you're helping to nurse a patient in Number Three."

"'Yes."

"'Does that patient require much attention?"

"'Not very much."

"'But you stay in the room?"

"'Oh, yes."

"'Do you draw the curtains at night?"

"'Yes."

"'Where do you sit in the room?"

"'In a corner close to the bed."

"'Close to the window, too?"

"'Yes, but the curtains are drawn."

"'But you move about, Sister Josephine?"

"'Oh, yes. But I'm sitting down for most of the time."

"'Do you ever look out on the terrace?"

"'I do sometimes while it's light. But at night the curtains are drawn."

"'Now please look back for a moment to Tuesday night. Between half past ten and two... Can you remember hearing any sound which was unusual – a sound, for instance, which you had not heard the night before?"

"'Oh, no, indeed."

"'Quite sure, Sister Josephine?"

"'Yes, I'm quite sure."

"'It's very important – this. You see, I'm almost sure that a sound *was* made or that a light *was* shown on the terrace during that night."

'The girl shook her head.

'"Does that mean you can't help me?"

'"Yes."

'There was a little silence.

'In the ordinary way I should have left it there. But I wasn't satisfied. Her last two answers seemed strange. The first two were so emphatic: but not the third. And I thought she protested too much that the curtains were drawn. Again, sweet face or no, she would not meet my eyes. If only the Mother Superior hadn't been there... Her presence embarrassed *me,* and I knew I was not at my best. Question and answer had been an exercise – the very thing I always seek to avoid.

'"Listen to me, Sister Josephine. In this very serious case, I must have everyone's help. Time and again in my life, I have discovered something of which I should have been told. And when I say to the person who should have told me, 'Why didn't you tell me that?' they say, 'Because you never asked me.' That answer always upsets me, for it means they've been strict with me. Of course, I should have asked them – the fault was mine: but we're all human, you know; and, though I do my best, I make a lot of mistakes. But if people help me, I don't make quite so many. So please don't be strict with me, and don't withhold the answer to a question I've failed to ask.'

'She looked up there for a moment. Then

she looked down and away.

""You were on duty for six hours?"

""Yes. From eight till two."

""Were you visited during that time?"

""Yes, by the House Surgeon."

""How many times did he come?"

""Twice."

""When did he come for the second time?"

""At about a quarter to ten."

""Were you visited by anyone else?"

""Yes. By Sister Helena."

""How many times by Sister Helena?"

""Three times, I think."

""Tell me about them, please?"

""The first was when she first came on, soon after eight. Then when I rang for her about a quarter to nine. And then she looked in, as usual, I think about ten o'clock."

""Did anyone else come in?"

""Sister Thérèse relieved me."

""Of course. But nobody else?"

""Oh, no."

""Sister Helena looked in, as usual, about ten o'clock?"

""Yes."

""She looks in from the terrace?"

""Yes."

""Does she part the curtains and just put in her head?"

""If I'm not at the window, she does."

""But you don't look out at night."

""No, but I hear her coming; and if I'm

not with my patient, I always get up."

"'And go to the window?"

"'Yes."

"'To be ready to greet her?"

"'Yes."

"'You hear her coming?"

"'Yes. Or I see the light of her torch."

"'Shining beneath the curtains?"

"'Yes."

"'Does she make much noise?"

"'Oh, no, she's very quiet."

"'Still, you can hear her coming?"

"'Usually, yes."

"'And she always parts the curtains and sometimes puts in her head?"

"'Yes."

"'Do you hear her go back?"

"'Yes."

"'Did you hear her come and go back on Tuesday night?"

"'Yes."

"'That was about ten o'clock?"

"'Yes."

"'And you didn't hear her again?"

"'No."

"'Or see her light?"

"'No."

"'She might have gone by, you know, without looking in."

"'I don't think she did."

"'And you saw or heard no one else?"

'Sister Josephine shook her head.

"'All right. Thank you."

'As the Mother Superior dismissed her–

"'Tell Sister Thérèse to come in."

'Sister Thérèse was quiet, but self-possessed. A grave, wise face. I liked her at once. I asked her much the same questions, and she gave me intelligent replies. I pressed her hard upon what she had seen and heard between two and four. She had seen Sister Helena first at a quarter past two. That was because she had rung. She had needed assistance upon a routine job. They had been, say, ten minutes together. Sister Helena had come and gone by the door. She had seen her again about three. On that occasion Sister Helena had parted the curtains and just looked into the room. She had looked up and nodded, and Sister Helena had gone. And that was all. No other movement or light – so far as she heard or saw.

'It was she Sister Helena called, when she found St Amant dead. She bore out in every particular what Sister Helena had said.

"'You had to leave your patient?"

"'Yes. But I had injected morphia only ten minutes before."

"'So he would require no attention for a quarter of an hour?"

"'It was very unlikely that he would. And this was an emergency."

"'Exactly. Well, thank you very much."

'As the door closed behind her–

101

"'A different type,' said the Mother Superior.

"'Very,' said I.

"'You have the impression that Sister Josephine could have said more than she did.'

"'To be honest, I have.'

"'I have that impression, too. We may be wrong, Superintendent, for Sister Josephine is a very saintly girl. Her devotion to duty is fanatic. But she dare not think for herself. She seeks divine guidance upon the most everyday things. Such guidance is not vouchsafed. So she has to fall back on the brain which she is afraid to use. Sometimes, as you may believe, with unhappy results. But, if you would like me to, I will have a talk with her.'

"'Madam,' I said, "I should be grateful indeed.'

"'Very well. Is there anything else you want?'

"'I have no doubt that visitors are allowed. I should like to know what visits were recently paid to Numbers One to Six.'

"'Pray see the porteress. She keeps the register.'

"'I am greatly obliged, madam.'

'With that, I took my leave.

'I confess I felt greatly relieved. If Dracona, as Dallas calls her, meant to co-operate, my chances of getting somewhere were considerably increased. And it looked as if she did. "We may be wrong, Superintendent." Well, those were friendly words. And then she had offered to tackle the girl, herself. In such a case, she could learn more in five minutes than I could learn in five hours.'

'I give you best, Falcon,' said Mansel. 'To reduce such a fortress as that was a triumph, indeed.'

Falcon regarded Jenny.

'Colonel Mansel, himself, would have done it in half the time.'

'I believe he would,' said Jenny. 'But then he's exceptional.'

'Now, now,' said Mansel, laughing.

'As a matter of fact,' said I, 'they're both of them right. I've seen you charm hostility into goodwill.' I looked at Falcon. 'It's like a conjuring trick. I've seen it many a time, but I never know how it's done. And now go on, Superintendent.'

'Well, before I did anything else, I visited Dallas again. That Sister Josephine had, in fact, heard or seen something, I now had no doubt. I believed she had heard a footfall. Now Dallas had seen his flash at a quarter to two. I was sure he'd been waked by the footfall which Sister Josephine heard.

'When I put my head into his room—

'"Now isn't that nice?" said Dallas, and offered me cigarettes.

'I lighted one and sat down.

'"How's your knee going on?"

'"The pain is less, Superintendent. You've

done me good."

"'I should like to think that, Mr Dallas."

"'You have indeed. Before you came, my plight obsessed my mind: but now my mind is otherwise occupied. Believe me, I'm with you in spirit in all you do. But you didn't come in to learn that."

"'No, I didn't,' I said. "The time when you saw that flash – are you sure it was a quarter to two?"

"'Of that, I'm quite sure."

"'I don't think a flash would have waked you."

"'Oh, no. It was something else. Almost certainly a sound. As I said, perhaps a footfall."

"'Sister Helena always comes round at about three o'clock."

"'I didn't know that."

"'She does. And she uses the terrace."

"'She's never waked me yet. But then she moves very quietly. Besides, I saw my flash at a quarter to two."

"'When you saw it, did you think it was her?"

"'I can't tell you what I thought. I was half asleep. I know that I saw a flash and I know that I saw that flash at a quarter to two."

"'How long had you been asleep?"

"'Getting on for three hours. I usually get to sleep about eleven o'clock."

"'What about St Amant? Did he say when

he went to sleep?"

'Dallas considered.

'"I don't think he did. We did compare notes, of course. But I don't think he told me that. But he went to sleep later than I did, for when I turned out my light, I think his was always on."

'"How could you tell?"

'"I could see the faint glow on the terrace. Placed as I am, I can't see the section of terrace in front of his room: but I can see the section of terrace belonging to his."

'"I understand. The glow must be very faint."

'"It is – or was very faint. And yet, when my light was out, quite easy to see. And one notices things, you know, lying here like this."

'"That's natural enough. Did you wake this morning at four?"

'"I did."

'"As usual."

'"As usual. For some extraordinary reason, the pain reports for duty at four o'clock. St Amant was just the same. But I told you that."

'"Did he keep his tablets till then?"

'"I remember his saying he did. He didn't like taking drugs and neither do I. Men don't, you know, Superintendent. I'll lay you don't take aspirin once a year."

'"I don't think I do."

'"Well, there you are. The woman's outlook

is different. Drugs, admittedly mild, are her staple food. And now it's coming back. I remember his saying, 'I don't like taking a drug to send me to sleep. If you start that sort of thing, you may have to go on.' And I agreed with him. No doubt that was why his light was on so late. He wouldn't take his tablets to send him to sleep. He kept them till four o'clock, to flatten the pain."

"'It looks like that," I said. I got to my feet. "Well, thank you very much."

"'To thank me," said Dallas, "is indecent – and you know it as well as I. The kick I get out of your visits will hardly go into words. *Au revoir,* Superintendent."

"'*Au revoir,*" I said, laughing.

'Then I went to the lodge and saw the porteress.

'She showed me The Visitors' Book. This is a proper register. Date; name and address of visitor; name of patient; relation of visitor to patient. No visitors for St Amant; but that I'd been told. Berryman's mother came to see him on Saturday last. Number One's daughter, on Monday; and on the same day the old Civil Servant's son. Only one entry made me think. A Madame de Porphyry came to see Dallas on Sunday – address The Savoy Hotel. She was entered as "Friend". I asked the porteress if she remembered her.

"'Yes," she said, "I do. She was very French."

'"Young?" I said.

'"Perhaps about forty," she said.

'"I don't think you liked her very much."

'"I'm afraid I didn't. When I asked her to register, she asked if this was a gaol."

'"I find that inexcusable."

'"Sister Geneviève will tell you more."

'"I haven't seen her today."

'"She'll be on duty again at four o'clock."

'"One more question, please. Did you see the Frenchwoman's car?"

'"Yes, it was a Rolls-Royce."

'"Colour?"

'"Black."

'"I see. Was she driving herself?"

'"No. She had a chauffeur."

'"I see. Well, thank you very much. Perhaps I shall want to look at that register again."

'"Whenever you please."

'It was then ten minutes to four, so I strolled to the gate and back. Then I entered the house and found Sister Geneviève.

'"Can you spare me ten minutes?" I said.

'"Yes, Superintendent. Would you mind if we talked on the terrace? Then the Sister in Number Three will tell me if anyone rings."

'"What could be better?" I said.

'We reached the terrace by way of St Amant's room.

'I glanced at Dallas' windows.

'"I don't want Number Five to hear what we say."

'"Let's go to the other end. One moment. I must just warn the Sister in Number Three."

'When she returned–

'"Was that Sister Josephine?"

'"No. She comes on at eight. Have you been questioning her?"

'"Yes," I said. "I wish she was as helpful as you."

'"She's very unworldly. I'm sure she tried her best."

'"Entirely between you and me, I'm not quite sure that she did."

'Sister Geneviève looked greatly surprised.

'"You amaze me, Superintendent."

'"There was something she didn't tell me."

'"That happened on Tuesday night?"

'"Yes. It may be of no importance, but I want to know what it was."

'"I'll see what I can do."

'I looked at her.

'"I don't wonder that Lord Amant called you St Geneviève. But, Sister Geneviève, this is between you and me – and nobody else."

'"That's understood, Superintendent." She drew in her breath. 'I oughtn't to say this, of course. But I want you to be successful in – in what you're trying to do."

Falcon stopped there, and a hand went up to his head.

'I suppose I was right to broach the matter to her. I acted on impulse. It never entered my head, until she said she must warn the Sister in Number Three. If the Mother Superior hears, she'll write me off. I suppose, in a sense, I am going behind her back. But Sister Josephine is afraid of her. That fear may command her answers. But no one could be afraid of Sister Geneviève. Besides, she'll be very skilful... I don't know what to think. However, it's done now.'

'I'm sure you were right,' said Mansel.

'So'm I,' said I. 'I used to act on impulse – and I never remember regretting what I had done. If you ask me, the girl was rattled. There was something she dared not say, in case the Mother Superior shouldn't approve. If I am right, your absence is not going to do any good. Sister Geneviève is very much more likely to get at the truth.'

'I entirely agree,' said Mansel. 'You must be glad of that woman.'

'I am, indeed,' said Falcon. 'For the Mother Superior, I have a profound respect. And we're now on very good terms. But I've something approaching affection for Sister Geneviève. There's something she didn't put off, when she took the veil. And I haven't done with her yet. Just listen to this.

'"And now," I said, "just a word about something else. Mr Dallas was visited, Sister, on Sunday last."

'"Yes," she said. "By a Frenchwoman – very French."

"'Who doesn't seem to have been very popular.'"

"'Her manners left much to be desired.'"

"'Why do you say that, Sister?'"

"'Well, she entered the corridor, as I came out of a room. I went to meet her at once. 'Take me to Mr Dallas,' was all she said. My hands were full, so I asked her to wait a moment. I went to my pantry and came back as soon as I could. That was in less than a minute. But she was gone. I went directly to Mr Dallas' room. Sure enough, there she was. She said something in French, and I saw Mr Dallas frown. Then she said in English, 'You see I have found my way without your help.' I didn't answer her, but I said to Mr Dallas, 'Will you ring, please, when the lady is ready to leave?' And he was very polite, as he always is. 'I promise I will,' he said.

"'He has very pleasant manners,' I said.

"'Yes, he is very nice. He always thanks us so nicely for all we do.'"

"'And Mr Berryman?'"

Sister Geneviève looked down.

"'He seems very embittered,' she said. "As cripples sometimes are.'"

"'But he's not a cripple?' I said.

"'Oh, no. I only meant that cripples are sometimes embittered. But he has no such excuse.'"

"'Does he ever thank you?' I said.

"'No. But there's no reason why he should."

"'That is a matter of opinion, Sister Geneviève."

"'And his mother is such a sweet woman. She thanked me with tears in her eyes."

"'He must be a great grief to her."

"'I fear he must."

"'Cast your mind back to yesterday morning. He says that he was quite sure that something was wrong; but that when he asked you what it was, you wouldn't talk."

"'That's quite true. I didn't want to tell him that Lord St Amant was dead."

"'Why not, Sister Geneviève?"

"'Because I was sure he would make some hateful remark. And I felt that I couldn't bear it, because Lord St Amant was – well, every single thing that a gentleman ought to be. We were so proud and happy to have him in our care."

"'I can well believe it," said I.

"'And he was so gay. He used to make the Mother Superior smile."

"'I think, perhaps, not many patients do that."

"'Not very many: they stand in awe of her. But he never did. He used to speak French with her. I don't know what he said, but one day she laughed outright."

"'I saw him once with Queen Mary, and she was shaking with laughter at something

111

he'd said."

"'We might have been queens, the way he treated us.'"

"'I'm sure of that. Well, thank you very much." As I said that, a hand went up to her mouth. "Yes," I said, "please tell me."

"'There's just one thing, Superintendent. I was going to tell you just now, but we passed on to something else. The Frenchwoman. You remember I said that I asked her to wait a minute, but that, when I got back, she was in Mr Dallas' room.'"

"'Yes.'"

"'Well, a little later I visited Lord St Amant, to take his tea-tray away. When I'd shut the door behind me, 'And what,' he said, 'is the Duchess doing here?' I didn't know what he meant, and told him so. He said, 'Ten minutes ago, a French lady of high degree burst into this room. I don't know who she wanted, but I'm sure that it wasn't me. She withdrew – precipitately.'"

"'They'd met before, Sister?'"

"'That's the impression I got.'"

"'What did you say?'"

"'I said I was terribly sorry and told him what had occurred. 'I shouldn't have left her,' I said. He smiled his charming smile. Then he said so gently, 'St Geneviève, when you apologize, it makes the angels weep.'

'She put her hand to her cheek and whipped away a tear.

'"Rubbish, of course," she said. "But it was such very sweet rubbish."

'I don't mind admitting that the tears came into my eyes...

'Then–

'"Anything more," I said.

'"I think that's all."

'I left the Convent then.

'I went to the station and dictated another report. Then I called on the Coroner. I gave him the statements, with which he seemed satisfied. The local superintendent will give him the rest. His summonses had been served that afternoon.

'"You'll keep me informed," he said.

'"I certainly will."

'"A difficult case, Superintendent."

'"It's not plain sailing," I said.

'"And the analysis?"

'"I hope for some news tomorrow. You'll be the first to hear. I don't expect to receive it before the afternoon. But even if it came in the morning, it couldn't be proved at the hearing tomorrow afternoon. What will be proved is that an analysis is being made. That can mean only one thing – that we suspect that Lord St Amant was poisoned. I think we shall have to consider when to release the result."

'"I leave it to you, Superintendent."

'"Thank you. I thought you would."

'I visited the station again, had a word

with Rogers and then drove here.

'Then, as you know, Rogers and I played about in the meadows last night. With your binocular, I could see clean into the rooms. I saw Sister Helena enter Dallas' room, with his spoon in her hand, and set it down by his side. Then I ventured on to the terrace. I walked right along by the parapet, and though both Dallas and Berryman were still awake, neither gave any sign of hearing or seeing me. From there, of course, I could see as much as I pleased.

'Before I forget, Mr Chandos, when Bell called me this morning, I gave him your binocular back.'

'Thank you, Superintendent. You'll say if you want it again.'

'I will, indeed.'

'Well now, before relating what happened today, I'd like to sum up.

'We've dealt with Berryman. Who shall we deal with next?'

'Dallas,' said Mansel.

'Exactly,' said Falcon. 'Now I'm almost certain that Dallas has told me the truth. But, though he was gossiping, he knew as well as did I, that he was laying a halter round Berryman's neck. Not sufficiently stout to hang him; but a halter, nevertheless. I have known that done by persons whose hands were not clean. The red herring, you know. And Dallas is nobody's fool. Now for his visitor. I don't know who she is, but I shall very soon. Did she tell Dallas or not that St Amant was lying next door? If she did, then Dallas has lied. But if Dallas has lied to me, then he's done it remarkably well. I find it rather hard to make up my mind, because I like the fellow – and that's the truth. Of course, he's terribly clever – no doubt about that. And though he can be very charming, he is not admirable. But no, I cannot see Dallas consenting to St Amant's death.'

Mansel raised his eyebrows.

'It is written,' he said, 'that one may smile and smile, and be a villain.' Still, from what you tell me, Falcon, I think you can – not rule out Dallas, but lay him aside. That he couldn't have done it himself is understood: but he might have consented. And now for the Duchess.'

'Ah,' said Falcon. 'I must confess I never expected her. And she seems to be a very unpleasant type.'

'I know just what she's like,' said Mansel. 'Better bred than some – with a vicious streak. Hard as nails. Rich on the money that she has extracted from men. Offensive to people for whom she has no use. Treating servants like dirt. And – dangerous. And she has failed with St Amant. They weren't on speaking terms. I don't wonder you're looking at her. And London will very soon know if she drives a grey car. Falcon, you're getting on.'

'Why "Madame de Porphyry"?'

'I've no idea. There must be some reason, of course: but it may be innocent. There isn't a *Duchesse de Porphyry* – that I know.'

'Quick work,' said Falcon. 'She obviously didn't know that St Amant was there.'

'Very quick work,' said Mansel. 'I give you that. *Veni, vidi, necavi.* But it could have been done. Reconnaissance on Monday. I know why you're hanging back.'

'Why?' said Falcon.

'Because she's too good to be true.'

'You're perfectly right, Colonel Mansel. She belongs to detective fiction.'

'What are you going to say if she drives a grey car?' Falcon laughed.

'Let me admit,' he said, 'that I've turned on the heat. If she's still in London, by now she is being watched. Her biography should be awaiting me when I get back. All the same, I like Berryman best. Finally, what can it be that Sister Josephine knows?'

'As like as not,' said I, 'it's insignificant. From the Mother Superior's estimate of the girl, to distinguish grain from chaff is beyond her power.'

'But she's holding out on me, Mr Chandos.'

'I know. A girl like that will tread the path of duty with bleeding feet. Then she comes to a place where the path of duty forks. She looks in vain for a signpost, to tell her which way to go. Only her brain can tell her, and that she's afraid to use. And that kind of girl will always choose the wrong way. Supposing she'd been on duty when St Amant had been found dead. And Sister Helena had called upon her, instead of on Sister Therèse. I'll lay you any money she wouldn't have left her patient. A conflict of duties. And she would have chosen wrong.'

'That's perfectly true.'

'It's on your mind,' said Mansel. 'If I were placed as you are, I think it would be on mine. But I think you should try to forget it. If the Mother Superior fails, Sister Geneviève should succeed in unlocking her tongue.'

'You're right. It's foolish to worry. I'll probably know tomorrow. The Mother Superior's asked me to come to her room at half past ten. May I lunch here, Mrs Chandos?'

'Superintendent, what do you think?'

'You're very sweet. I'd hoped to get off before lunch. But I've got so much to see to, before I go, that I've told them not to expect me till four o'clock. That means I shall sleep at my flat and leave on Sunday morning for Curfew Place.

'And so we come to Friday – that is to say, today.

'The first thing I did was to examine the meadows in which we had moved last night. I thought the grass might show traces of

117

where we had been. Not one remained.

'Then I drove to the Station. I saw the Chief Constable there and the local police. I told them – not all I've told you, but as much, to be perfectly frank, as I thought they should know. I've known indiscretions committed. Some years ago, a local Inspector saved a murderer's life. And I don't want an accident here. But here they've been very nice. No jealousy of the Yard, and always ready to help.

'The Chief Constable said this morning–

'"We don't seem to be doing much."

'"For the moment, sir, outside the Home, there's very little to do."

'"Well, don't forget that we're always at your disposal, day and night."

'"You don't have to tell me that, sir."

'Then we discussed the Inquest. I said that I should be there, but should not interfere.

'"I know my limitations. Superintendent Holer will do it much better than I. And now tell me this. The Coroner's out to help, and I'm sure that he will. How does he deal with his juries?'

'The local superintendent smiled.

'"They'll do as he tells them, sir. He's very strict."

'"Questions?"

'"No. It's got to be a very good question, for him to allow. And then, nine times out of ten, he'll answer it himself."

'"Then that's all right."

Falcon looked round.

'This was a great relief. A Coroner's jury can be a thorn in the flesh.

'"What about the Press, Superintendent?"

'"Make everything smooth for them, but don't say a word. Say that I'll see them this evening at six o'clock. Now tell me about the Court. Is there more than one way in?"

'"There's the Coroner's private door."

'"I'd rather not use that."

'"There's a passage from the mortuary yard."

'"I expect the gates of the yard are high, blind doors."

'"They are that, sir."

'"Then that will do very well. Please have two men on the gates, one inside and one out. When the one outside sees my car coming, he knocks on the gate: that tells the one inside to open the leaves. And they shut the gates behind me, directly I'm in."

'"That shall be done, Superintendent."

'"I'll hang on my heel at the Station, if you'll have an officer waiting to show me the way."

'So it was all arranged.

'Then I had a word with the Yard. They said the analysis was done and that I should receive the report this afternoon.

'Rogers had found nothing out from the Convent staff. To tell the truth, I never expected he would. Not his fault. I've little doubt that gossip is sternly discouraged: and when servants aren't permitted to gossip, they soon stop noticing things. It's no good collecting material which you can never use.

'Then St Amant's solicitor arrived, and we had a short talk. He was really extremely nice. Fenton, of Fenton and Clowes. Deeply shocked, of course. "I simply can't understand it. I wouldn't have thought he'd an enemy in the world. I'm so thankful it's in your hands. Anything we can do, you've only to let us know."

'"Tell me of Curfew Place. I hope to be there on Sunday. Who shall I find in charge?"

'"You'll find George Selden there. He and St Amant have lived together for years. St Amant's right-hand man. He was always in charge, if St Amant went away. And he knew St Amant better than anyone else. Major The Honourable George Selden. Mad about horses of course, as St Amant was. The latter went out and about, as of course you know. But Selden never stirred. You might get something from him, for I think he'll talk to you."

'"I hope you're right. Can you tell me about the Will?"

'"I've a copy here, Superintendent. It's simple enough."

'I read it through.

'Curfew Place, as it stands, goes to George Selden for life with five thousand a year. His stables to three Trustees, of whom George Selden is one: and fifty thousand with them. The establishment to be gradually reduced, with as little hardship as possible to man or beast: Selden's advice to be honoured on every point. The residue goes to his heir. Certain legacies to servants.

'As I handed the document back–

'"Then Curfew Place," I said, "was not entailed."

'"Oh, no. It isn't a seat. He bought it in '45. The family place is near Oakham. It's been let to Sir Arthur Lackland for several years."

'"I see. And the heir?"

'"His cousin. A very decent fellow, rather shy. Rather older than Lord St Amant. A widower with two boys. He's on his way back now."

'"Well-to-do?"

'"Yes. His wife was a very rich girl."

'I got to my feet.

'"Well, thank you very much."

'"Er, about the funeral, Superintendent. I was hoping perhaps we could have it on Monday next."

'"I'm sure you can," I said. "But that's not a matter for me. I should see the Coroner this morning."

'"May I say that you've no objection?"

'"Yes, indeed."

'"He'll be buried at Curfew, of course. I think it should be most private. A memorial service later."

'"I should think that would be best."

'Then Paterson rang up.

'"Are you coming this morning, Superintendent?"

'"I was coming to see you," I said. "Why do you ask?"

'"It's nothing of importance," he said, "but the Mother Superior has her solicitor here."

'"She'd like me to meet him?" I said.

'"Yes."

'"In half an hour's time," I said…

'I tied up a few more ends. Then I took the car and drove to the Home.

'I was taken at once to the Mother Superior's room.

'I must say she spoke very nicely.

'"Superintendent, this is my solicitor, Mr Bateman. I have been telling him how fortunate we find it that you are in charge of this case."

'"That's very kind of you, madam."

'"I mean what I say. And now I have things to attend to; so will you talk together in a consulting-room?"

'So off we went.

'Bateman, I should say, is an excellent business man. But in a matter like this he was out of his depth. And he was much too wise to try to cover it up. He was very deferential. Would I mind if he came to the Inquest?

"'Mr Bateman,' I said, "it's right that you should be there. But I hope you won't ask any questions – I mean, at this stage."

"'Indeed, I shan't, Superintendent. From what my client says, it would be an impertinence."

"'You mustn't feel that. As representing the Home, you would be within your rights. But just for today, I hope you'll reserve any points and make them to me later on."

"'That's very kind of you. But matters like this, Superintendent, are not in my line."

"'I know. But you have a legal mind. And in a case like this I want all the help I can get. I've really nothing to tell you that you don't know. I suspect that Lord St Amant was poisoned. Whether he was or was not, I shall know tonight. Dr Paterson will be told, as soon as I have the news. If he was poisoned, it cannot have been accidental: and I am perfectly sure that he didn't poison himself."

"'A shocking thing, Superintendent."

"'From every point of view."

'Bateman lowered his voice.

"'Er, if I may say so, Superintendent, you've handled the Mother Superior wonderfully well. She speaks most cordially of you. And that, you must take it from me, is a tribute indeed. She's a wonderful woman, you know. But terribly jealous of her prerogative. I don't know how you've done it, but you have won her respect."

"'I'm very glad, if I have, if for no other reason, because I respect her so much. I mean, she's been spared nothing. Lord St Amant was always what is called 'news'. And now he has died by the administration of poison, while in her charge. Such a disaster must have hit her between the eyes. A knock-out blow, Mr Bateman. And she has met it, as though it were a flick on the chin. She commands my great admiration – and that is the truth."

'We parted on excellent terms, and I asked for Paterson.

'He came in a minute or two.

"'Three things only," I said. "First, the result of the analysis should be in my hands by five. If poison has been found, I shall ring you up. I shan't discuss the matter: the fact that I ring you up will mean that it has been found."

"'I quite understand."

"'Secondly, tell me this. You're the House Surgeon here; but have you no assistant?"

"'I have, but he is on leave. I had a wire today, asking if he should return. I propose to say no. He's in the South of France."

"'When did he start his leave?"

"'A fortnight ago on Sunday."

"'Isn't the work here too much for one man?"

"'Not as a rule. Take the rooms on the terrace. There's only one man there that I have to watch. And I can do little more than the sisters do. His specialist comes to see him twice a week."

"'But you're always at hand."

"'Oh, yes. But I don't mind that. I'm very well lodged and looked after. When you have time, you must come and see my house."

"'I'd like to. Now for the third thing. Did you see the woman who visited Dallas on Sunday?"

'Paterson shook his head.

"'I didn't know that he'd had a visitor."

'I told him some of what I had learned.

"'French?" he said. "I know that he lives in France."

'I shrugged my shoulders.

"'There's probably nothing in it. I think that's all. Will you make your own way to the Court?"

"'I think perhaps I'd better."

"'The local superintendent will be in charge."

"'Holer. I know him, of course. He's a very decent chap."

"'And I shall be in the background."

"'I'm glad of that. You're going to take Sister Helena?"

"'Yes."

"'I'm glad of that, too."

"'D'you know who's coming with her?"

"'I've no idea. Sister Claude, I should think. She's played duenna before."

'I drove to *The Crown* for lunch, but the Press had taken possession and I could hardly get in. They fell upon me, of course. 'Nonsense,' I said. 'You don't want me to-day.' 'We always want you,' and so on. 'I think you've enough with the Inquest, but if you like, I'll see you at six o'clock.' 'That's good enough, Superintendent.' A meal there was out of the question, so I got Rogers out of his room and we drove to the Station forthwith. They sent out for some food for us, and we really did very well.

'Afterwards, Rogers and I had a little talk. I told him about the Frenchwoman and set him the thankless task of checking the line which the grey car had taken on Monday or, possibly, Tuesday night. As a matter of fact, if she was driving that car, it shouldn't be very hard. He'll work on that while I'm away.

'Then I spoke about something else.

'"Rogers," I said, "I've left you alone a lot, but you mustn't think I want this case to myself."

'"Never entered my head, Super."

'"Well, that's all right. But I want you to understand that, so far as the Convent's concerned, this is a one-man job."

'"You're telling me, sir," says Rogers. "And now I'll tell you something. I know where I get off, and I'm better outside those gates. And I'm very glad to think that you're sleeping away, for there's nowhere at all to sit, except in the bar. That's all right for me, for they talk to me at night, as they'd never have talked to you. You see, you're too well known. But I've picked up bits and pieces, and they're going in my report.'

'"Well, that's all right," I said. "So long as you understand."

'"No call to say that, Super. We've worked together too long."

'At a quarter past one we left for the Nursing Home. We took two cars. Rogers knew what to do. He drove himself, but I had a driver with me.

'When I looked at the porteress—

'"Consulting-room B," she said.

'I knocked on the door. Sister Helena opened this.

'"Ready?" I said, smiling.

'"I think so," she said and stepped back.

'Her companion rose to her feet.

'It was the Mother Superior.

'"We are ready, Superintendent," she said.

'I could only bow. I don't think I could have spoken, if I had known what to say. I was honestly overcome. I remembered Paterson's words. *She loves her flock.* Well, this was love. For this great lady, this Abbess, this almost legendary figure was going like some humble sister to share with one of her children that child's ordeal. She could have sent whom she pleased. But no, she must go herself, to endure the vulgar surroundings, to court the stares of the morbid and the hungry gaze of the Press... I felt that was truly great.'

'So it was,' said Mansel. 'And not only great. It was the way of Christ. My God, what it must have cost her!'

'I know,' said Falcon. 'I can't remember when I've been so much moved.

'I stood back for them to pass...

'The blinds of both cars were drawn. They entered mine. Before I shut the door–

'"Madam," I said, "I beg that you will stay in the car, until I, and nobody else, ask you to alight."

'"Very well, Superintendent. Thank you."

'Rogers took my seat by the driver, and I took the wheel of his car and led the way...

'A constable was waiting at the Station and took his seat by my side. He told me the way to go, and the other car followed behind.

'A crowd was surging about the door of the Court. But the gates of the yard came first. As we approached, I saw them begin to open.

'"You're passing it, sir," cried the constable.

'"That's all right," I said, with my eyes on the mirror above.

'I saw my car disappear.

'As I drew up to the Court, I saw the cameras... All eyes were fast upon me, and I fancy that very few people had noticed the second car. I took my time getting out, and as I made for the steps, Rogers came quietly up and took my place at the wheel.

'I passed through the dingy hall, down a passage and into the Mortuary Yard. I told the driver to have the car turned and ready before I came back. Then I opened the door, and the two got out.

'Rogers waited two minutes before he drove off. And the Press waited with him. If you remember, the blinds of his car were drawn. By the time he let in his clutch, I had the ladies comfortably settled in Court.

'I won't describe the inquest. The Coroner did it well. Sister Helena's demeanour was perfect. Her appearance caused a sensation – when she entered the box, I mean. I can't say that I was surprised. Till then she had kept her head bowed: but then she held it up. Raphael, perhaps, could have caught the purity of her features and the blue and white of her robes. And that very sweet, low voice... She never faltered once, and I heard every single word. Paterson gave his evidence very well. Throughout the proceedings, the silence in Court was most remarkable. No rustle, not a murmur, until a witness stood down. Then everyone seemed to relax...

'And then, at last, it was over.

'They got away as they had come: but this time I sat in front. Rogers was outside the Court with an empty car and a constable standing beside it. When he saw me leave the yard, he followed behind. So we escaped attention. But I have an uneasy feeling that we shan't be so lucky again.

'When we reached the Home, I saw them out of the car and into the hall.

'There the Mother Superior turned and put out her hand.

'"Superintendent," she said, "we are very deep in your debt." I took her fingers and bowed. "Can you spare me ten minutes tomorrow – at, shall we say, half past ten?"

'"I shall be here, madam."

'Then both of them bowed very sweetly and I withdrew.

'I entered Rogers' car and we drove to the Station at once. The other car followed behind.

'The result of the analysis was there. I should have told you before that they've set apart an office for Rogers and me to use. I opened the envelope there.

'With the official report was a letter from Sir William himself, saying in very plain terms exactly what we wanted to know. No medical jargon, I mean.'

Falcon's hand went to his pocket and drew out a foolscap sheet.

'I've got it here, and I'll read you what it says.

Lord St Amant was poisoned.

The poison administered was MAFRA – a little-known drug.

I first came across it in France in 1939. The

Sûreté, were worried about it. It seemed to be being supplied to well-bred Society women in tablet form. They didn't use it: but they knew that war was coming and they kept it ready in case things should go wrong. If a German should offer them violence, rather than suffer that, they could take their own lives. The dose was two white tablets – which I was shown.

MAFRA is very efficient. Death would be certain, painless and swift, say thirty to fifty seconds – no more than that. The actual time would depend on the state of the victim's heart. The dose was supplied in capsules – two tablets in each. It was said that saliva would not dissolve the capsule, which could therefore be concealed in the mouth and only swallowed if the worst should befall. I did not see such a capsule and I doubt such efficacy. MAFRA can still be procured in France, though not, of course, openly: and many ladies keep it in case the Russians should come. There are two or three cases on record of poisoning in this way. But this is the first case in England, so far as I know.'

There was a little silence.

Then–

'And that,' said Mansel, 'has shortened Madame de Porphyry's price.'

'I'll say it has,' said Falcon. 'She's favourite now. Still, the call-over isn't yet. And Berryman may come up.

'And now I'll just finish today, and then we'll talk.

131

'I rang up Paterson and made an appointment with him for eleven o'clock tomorrow. He knew what I meant.

'Then I called on the Coroner. I didn't mention this letter, but showed him the formal report. I said I proposed that the Press should be told on Monday, for I could see no reason for keeping it up our sleeve. "More. In such a case as this, we can't keep the public waiting for fully a week." He agreed reluctantly, for he would have liked to bring it out at the Inquest. Of course I was being civil: we don't have to have his permission to publish the fact.

'Then I went back to the Station and dictated a full report. While that was being typed, I saw the Press...

'I knew what was coming of course. "What was Sister Helena's surname?" I said that, whatever it was, it had been renounced. "Surely it should have been given." "Don't be silly," I said. "I remember a High Court Judge allowing a nun to bear witness as Sister X. Judge, Magistrate, Coroner – all have a wide discretion. And I think that both you and I would have thought the less of this Coroner if he had hurt such a lady in such a wanton way." So that finished that. Then they asked for news. "You may say this," said I. "That tomorrow afternoon I'm going back to the Yard. I can't do any more here for two or three days." "Are you following some line,

Superintendent?" "More than one." I said. "You're assuming Lord St Amant was murdered?" "I'm bound to do that. If I waited for the analysts' report, I might be wasting quite invaluable time. Scent grows cold, you know." "Was that the Mother Superior?" "Yes, it was." "Did she come at your request?" "Certainly not. I'd no idea she was coming, until I went to the Convent to pick Sister Helena up." "Can you tell us why she came?" "I'm afraid I haven't asked her," I said. "We didn't photograph them," said someone. "That was very forbearing," I said, and everyone laughed. "And now I can't say any more. But I'll give you a tip. Look out for Sunday evening. I can't be sure, but I think you'll have something then."

'Then I went back to the Station, to sign my report. And then I drove here.'

'Two fruitful days,' said Mansel. 'Honestly, Falcon, I don't think you can complain.'

'Indeed, I can't, Colonel Mansel. I think I've been very lucky. The pieces of the puzzle are mounting as I never thought they would. And I hope to hear tomorrow that Sister Josephine has opened her mouth.'

'I imagine you'll show that letter to no one at all.'

'To no one,' said Falcon. 'Not even to Paterson. That is the sort of letter one keeps very close.'

There was a little silence.

133

Then—

'Superintendent,' said Jenny, 'I don't want to speak out of turn.'

'You can never do that, Mrs Chandos. Please say whatever you please.'

'Well, I met Rosemary Vernon in 1938.'

'That,' said Falcon, 'is just what I wanted to know. I gave you her name, because Berryman brought it out. And so I was not committing a breach of confidence. But I purposely left it there, for I am not here as a policeman, but as a guest. But now you have broached the matter. Will you be so kind as to tell me what you remember of Lady Rosemary Vernon, now Sister Helena?'

'Richard was away,' said Jenny. 'Abroad with Jonathan. And I had gone to Buckram to stay for ten days with the Baldrics – they're terribly nice. And while I was there, Rosemary came with her sister for two or three days. She was only sixteen then, although she looked older than that. And she was simply lovely and awfully sweet. She and I were together most of the time – they used to call us "the children" – I've just remembered that. Rosemary was simply mad about horses and dogs. She said she hoped to be presented in 1939. She asked me all about Richard and how we lived. And then I remember her saying, "That's the life. A quiet home in the country with a husband you really love." I said, "I think so, too: but you'll have to go about." Then she said, "You don't look as if you'd done that, Jenny Chandos." So I told her how Richard had found me and carried me off.

'I can't remember very much more; but when she left, she kissed me and said, "We shall meet again. I'm coming to Maintenance one day, whether you ask me or not." But she never did, and I never saw her again.

'It was some time during the War that Natalie told me that she had become a nun. I simply couldn't believe it, but Natalie swore it was true. "Just went religious," she said. "It's been done before."

'That's all, I'm afraid, Superintendent.'

'It's quite a lot,' said Falcon. 'I was going to search the files of a paper or two. But I shouldn't have found an appreciation like that. I'm very grateful, Mrs Chandos. You've helped me more than you know.'

It was getting late by then, so after a very few minutes we went upstairs and bade one another goodnight.

When Jenny and I were alone–

'Darling,' she said, 'why did Rosemary take the veil?'

'Because,' I said, 'she was disappointed in love.'

'There!' said Jenny, and kissed me. 'That's what I've always felt. Are you going to tell Mr Falcon?'

'No, I'm not, my sweet – because Falcon

thinks so, too.'

On the following afternoon, Falcon was back for lunch, as he had said he should be. When coffee had been served on the terrace, he glanced at his watch.

'Plenty of time,' he said. 'I needn't leave here before three.' He looked round pleasedly. 'If I could do as I liked, I shouldn't leave here at all. A quiet weekend with you would suit me down to the ground.'

'I wish you could stay,' said Jenny. 'I think you must be tired.'

'When it's over, perhaps, Mrs Chandos.'

'We'll hold you to that,' said I.

'You won't have to hold me,' said Falcon. 'And now, if you'd like to hear, I'll tell you what happened this morning.'

'If you please.'

'I'll cut out the routine work and pass direct to the Home.

'The Mother Superior received me at half past ten. She smiled very pleasantly and asked me to take a seat. Then she went straight to the point.

'"I have seen Sister Josephine. We were perfectly right, Superintendent. She has confessed with tears what it was she failed to divulge. I'm afraid it's not very important, but whether or no it is, is for you to judge.

'"You will remember that you asked her what visits she had had: and that she replied

136

that she had been visited by the House Surgeon and by Sister Helena. And when you said 'Anyone else?', she replied "Sister Thérèse." Well, that meant that she was fencing, as both of us saw. So again you asked the same question, and she said no."

"'I remember perfectly, madam.'"

"'Well, now I must make a confession. I think I'll put it like this. As no doubt you have already surmised, I visit the patients myself. I usually pay my visits between five and six in the evening: sometimes I go in the morning, if I have time to spare. I can't visit every patient every day, because I have too much to do: but daily Dr Paterson renders me written reports. So, though I may not have seen them, I know how they're all going on. And if any patient is seriously ill, I may visit him or her twice, or more often than that.

"'As I think you know, Superintendent, the patient in Number Three is very seriously ill. I visited him in the morning, but on Tuesday I had no time to pay him a second visit between five and six.

"'At half past nine that evening, my day was nearly done. I had some letters to deal with, but that was all. I was writing my second letter, when it suddenly came to me that I had failed to revisit Number Three. So I rose and paid my visit there and then.

"'Mine was the visit, Superintendent, which Sister Josephine failed to disclose.

"'I don't know that she can be blamed. Had she been alone with you, she might or might not have disclosed it. But since you saw her in my presence, she felt that it was not for her to declare that I had been in.

"'So you see, Superintendent, the fault was mine. I fear I am growing forgetful – I'm not as young as I was. On Tuesday I nearly forgot to visit Number Three: and on Thursday I forgot that I had done so. I used not to do things like that."

"'Madam,' I said, 'you have many things to think of.'

"'Yes, I have. Still, one shouldn't forget. I'm glad to have cleared up the matter. I'm only sorry, Superintendent, that I should have been to blame.'

"'With respect, madam,' I said, 'I don't admit that you were. I can certainly see Sister Josephine's point of view. But a more sophisticated sister would have reminded you of the visit you paid.'

"'Of course she would. Almost any other sister would have done so. But, if you remember, I said that Sister Josephine was afraid to think for herself.'

"'Indeed, I remember, madam. I'm only so glad you've been able to clear it up. I'm always worried by something I can't understand.'

"'Of course you are. And now tell me this, Superintendent. Is it a fact that you're leaving the district today?"

"'It is, madam. I must go to London and then to Curfew Place."

"'I hope you won't be away long."

"'On Wednesday or Thursday, madam, I shall be back. Before then, if I'm summoned, of course. But I don't expect that. Chief Inspector Rogers will still be here. He is at your disposal. If you should wish to see him, you've only to ring up the police."

"'Thank you." She hesitated. Then, "I hope that you're making progress."

"'I think I can say that the case is not standing still. I can't pretend it's straightforward. In nine cases out of ten the police have something to go on. But this is the tenth. I've got to find something to go on, before I can start. It's always there, you know, if you've eyes to see. But this is one of those cases in which one needs very keen sight."

"'I fancy that's why you were sent." She sighed. "Our lives are very different: but I think we both do our duty with all our might. That is all that matters, Superintendent. The words Success and Failure are not written in the Book of Life."

"'I shall try to remember that, madam: because it is so true." I got to my feet. "And now I must take my leave."

"'Till Wednesday or Thursday, then. And thank you for all you've done."

"'That's very gracious, madam."

139

'"And more than you expected the first time we met."

'She was smiling and I smiled back.

'"Frankly, yes, madam."

'"You must thank yourself," she said.

'I bowed and withdrew.'

Falcon looked at me.

'So, you see, you were right, Mr Chandos. My hunch was wrong. Poor Sister Josephine. Her hesitation was natural. With the Mother Superior there, it needed more courage than she possessed to disclose a fact which the Mother Superior did not see fit to reveal.

'Then I saw Paterson and gave him the analysts' report. He read it carefully. Then he looked at me.

'"Mafra," he said. "I've never heard of Mafra. It must be extremely rare. And swift. Thirty to fifty seconds. He probably took it at four. I think he said that he used to wake up about then. Or it may have been Dallas. I've probably got it down in my reports."

'"May I see those reports some time?"

'"Of course. I make them out every day. The original sheets go to the Mother Superior: the copies stay in the book. Will it do, when you come back?"

'"Oh, yes. There's no hurry at all."

'"You must come to my house. Then you can go through them there."

'"That's an engagement," I said. "And now I must be going. Don't forget that Chief

Inspector Rogers is staying here. You've only got to ring up and he'll be along."

"'Thanks very much. I'll be glad to see you back. I can't get over that poison. Mafra. While you're away, I must do a little research."

'I drove back to Ne'er-do-well, where I saw the Chief Constable and the local police. I spent some time with them – one's got to be fair. Then I went through the papers. Sensational stuff, of course: but it might have been worse. Nothing that one could object to. Then I saw Rogers and told him to keep me informed.

'I think that's all.

'I'm afraid I forgot to say that I brought my driver with me. I handed him over to Bell. You must forgive me for that.'

Jenny smiled.

'You're forgiven, Superintendent. You've got so much to think of.'

For a moment Falcon sat silent, with his eyes on the middle distance. Then–

'Yes,' he said quietly. 'I have.'

It was natural enough that that evening we should review the case.

'Falcon,' said Mansel, 'is a most exceptional man. He has met with no end of success, as all of us know, and I'm sure that's due, partly to his very fine instinct, and partly to a remarkable ability to read the nature of man. His instinct, of course, is a gift; he was born with that. But he has taught himself to read the nature of man. And now he's a very great expert. Whenever he questions someone who might have been involved in some crime, he sets less store by their answers than by the impression they give. In other words, he is trying to capture their outlook. Some natures are as easy to read as an open book: others are most hard to decipher. Dallas' nature, for instance, is clearly most hard to read. And so is Paterson's. And don't forget this – that a clever, guilty man will always do his best to suppress those pages of his outlook which he doesn't want Falcon to read. And then, of course, it comes to a battle of brains.'

'Is that what he meant,' said Jenny, 'when he said he was looking for a needle in a bottle of hay?'

'Yes, my sweet. The motive was the needle, and the outlooks made up the hay. As a rule, the motive is apparent; and then you're half-way home. Only halfway, of course. A man is found robbed and murdered: well, the motive was clearly gain. Take the famous case of Oxen, whose wife had disappeared. It was perfectly clear that Oxen wished to be rid of his wife. But the murder was three months old, and no one but Falcon, I think, would have brought it home. But here the motive is hidden. Who on earth would wish or would dare to murder such a man as St Amant? A man whose charm was such that he could make such a Mother Superior laugh. Men like that are not murdered – in the ordinary way. Then again, whoever did it must have known that all the resources of the Law would be drawn on to find him out.'

'I agree,' said I. 'Falcon's terribly good, but he's up against something here. Madame de Porphyry looks very promising, and if she drives a grey car, she's going to be in a spot. But she may have an alibi. And, frankly, I can't see a woman going to work in such a methodical way. You or I would make a re-connaissance first, as a matter of course. But I find it hard to believe that a woman would.'

'What about Berryman?'

'He's well in the running,' said I. 'He sounds a spiteful brute and he may very well have been nursing some bitter grudge.'

'Consider it this way,' said Mansel. 'By the finding of Mafra, Sir William has given this case a very new look. The possession of such a poison is going to be most terribly hard to prove. And it's got to be proved, William. That Madame de Porphyry had it is highly probable. That's why she leads the field. But who's going to find the physician who sold it to her – when even the Sûreté can't trace transactions like that? If, say, she'd been seen on the terrace on Tuesday night, that fact would be so suspicious that her actual possession of Mafra might be assumed. Might. And the one japonica tablet which Falcon found might send her down. But she wasn't seen on the terrace.'

Jenny put in her oar.

'Supposing she gave it to Dallas.'

'Paterson says that Dallas can't put his foot to the ground.'

'I suppose,' said Jenny slowly, 'it couldn't have been a mistake. That somebody meant to murder Dallas, and went into Number Four, instead of Number Five.'

'That,' said Mansel, 'is humanly possible. And if every other line fails, Falcon may follow that up. But it's most unlikely, because the centre of the terrace lies between Three and Four. One can conceive a stranger confusing Three with Four: but Five is too far to one side. Besides, that's just the mistake against which a determined stranger would be on his guard.'

There was a little silence.

Then—

'There's just one point,' I said, 'which Falcon didn't make and we never raised.'

'I know, teacher,' said Mansel.

'I'm sure you do.'

'What is the point, darling?'

'This, my sweet. If Berryman recognized Lady Rosemary, it's Lombard Street to an orange that Lord St Amant did, too.'

'That's right,' said Mansel. 'It's rather

dramatic, really; though much the same sort of thing must have happened many a time during the first great war. In fact, I know it did. You found yourself being nursed by a girl that you had danced with two years before. Not quite the same, of course.'

'Oh, no. Not the same,' said Jenny. 'Because they weren't nuns. I mean, that would make it so awkward. What ever would they do?'

'I imagine he'd leave it to her. If she chose to recall their acquaintance, well and good.'

'I should have,' said Jenny.

'Of course you would, my sweet. You'd have had a glorious time. But then you would have forgotten that you were a nun.'

'I think it's all wrong,' said Jenny. 'It simply isn't natural. And it isn't what Rosemary wanted. She wanted to be like us. I suppose they got hold of her.'

'I've heard they do that,' said Mansel. 'You see, it's their belief that the girl who renounces the world becomes, as Falcon said, the Bride of Christ. And a higher honour than that no man can conceive.'

'It isn't natural,' said Jenny. 'And what isn't natural is wrong.'

I confess I agreed with her.

The fine weather broke on Sunday, and we had much wind and rain for the next two days. But Wednesday morning was clear, and as the day wore on, it grew very hot.

We had persuaded Mansel not to be gone.

'If for no other reason, you must see this out,' I said.

'Well, I must go next Monday,' he said. 'And I can't believe that it'll be over by then.'

'Once he gets a break,' said I, 'it may very well go very fast.'

'That's true. Did anything strike you, William, before Falcon went?'

'Just at the last,' I said, 'I thought he seemed rather thoughtful.'

'I thought so, too,' said Mansel. 'Well, we shall see.'

'Paterson?'

'Now why d'you say that?' said Mansel.

'Well, as we agreed just now, Falcon seemed rather thoughtful on Saturday afternoon. Well, that suggests that something had occurred that morning to make him think. Whom had he seen – not counting the Station crowd? The Mother Superior and Paterson. I know we can rule no one out, but if you're going to tell me that the Mother Superior did it – well, then, I withdraw.'

'No,' said Mansel, laughing, 'I'm not going to tell you that.'

'Well, that leaves Paterson. I'll lay Falcon watched him closely, while he was reading the report. You see, he could easily have done it. He was on the spot and he knew the ways of the Home. He knew the habits of the patients – he's said as much. And, as a doc-

146

tor, he could have procured the poison. Finally, who would suspect the House Surgeon himself?'

'Very true, William,' said Mansel. 'Your strongest card is the poison. Wash Madame de Porphyry out – and I don't fancy her – and who could have obtained Mafra ... at any time? It's been known for fifteen years – but not to the world. Sir William, a physician, knew it. He had been shown it in France. But he had been shown it, as a doctor. Well, Paterson may have been shown it – years ago ... and he may have been given two tablets, under seal. "May I take these?" "Yes, go on." Between physicians, you know. But his motive is not apparent.'

'Get at Paterson's history, and that might appear. Who sent St Amant to the Home?'

'The Yard will have found that out.'

That Wednesday we lunched with the Avons. As the Rolls slid up the beautiful avenue, Jenny cried out.

'Stop for a moment, darling. There! Just look at that.'

She knew Lockley better than I did. I might well have gone by.

The prospect was truly rare. A ride had been cut through the bracken, to stretch like an emerald carpet for more than a hundred yards. From that point, the ground went falling out of our view. On either hand, flanking the bracken, a mighty bulwark of foliage was turning the ride into a living bailey of great magnificence. And far in the distance, framed by forest and sky, a sparkle of blue and silver declared the open sea. Foliage, fronds and turf – all had been refreshed by the recent rain, and the setting seemed to belong to the days of chivalry. Almost one expected a light-hearted cavalcade to rise into view, moving slowly towards us with hawk and hound and laughter, lords and ladies and horses so pleased with life. I found it tragic indeed that the ninth Earl of Avon and Lippe, being two-thirds blind, had never felt the tug of this prospect for more than thirty-five years.

We were home soon after four, and as we were finishing tea, I thought I heard Falcon's voice.

Jenny, with Oakham behind her, was off in a flash.

As I came into the hall–

'Of course, Superintendent. Bell, you'll see to the driver. He's going to stay the night.'

'Very good, madam.'

'And please tell Mrs Tufton we want some fresh tea.'

'Very good, madam.'

I put out my hand.

'Superintendent, I'm glad to see you – and very glad indeed that you're here at four instead of at eight o'clock.'

Falcon smiled.

'Both you and Mrs Chandos spoil your guests. To be honest, I feel rather guilty, for I've cut out Ne'er-do-well. But I knew that if I went there, it would lengthen my day by two hours: and as I'm rather tired, I thought I'd give it a miss. That's why I brought my driver. You two are so good to me that I begin to presume.'

'But, you see, we like you,' said Jenny. 'And when it's all over, you're going to stay for a week. And we'll take you to Lockley: we've been there to luncheon today.'

'Isn't that Lord Avon's place?'

'Yes.'

'We were at Harrow together. I'd like to see him again. And now may I go and wash? And may I ask Bell to get through to Ne'er-do-well? I'd like to speak to Rogers...'

The call came through, as Falcon sat down to tea.

Carson appeared.

'You're through to the Station, sir.'

'Please excuse me, Mrs Chandos.' Falcon rose and turned. 'Oh, it's Carson. Carson, I'm very glad to see you again.'

'It's nice to see you, sir.'

As the door closed–

'Pressing my servant into your service,' said Mansel.

'I decline to believe that he needs any pressing,' I said. 'If he does, he's changed a lot in the last few years.'

149

'As a matter of fact,' said Jenny, 'he shares the duty with Bell.'

'And now you see,' I said, 'why we don't want to let you go.'

After a minute or two, Falcon came back. 'Well, that's all right,' he said. 'Nothing that cannot wait.'

'When you've had your tea,' said Jenny, 'you're coming to see the stables. And then we'll stroll in the meadows and you shall make friends with the sheep.'

'How did you know,' said Falcon, 'that that was what I wanted to do?'

'Well, it always refreshes me, and I thought you looked tired.'

'For the weary mind,' said Mansel, 'the Nursery Rhyme provides the perfect salve. Green meadows and mansions and sweet-smelling stalls, and the unaffected friendship of the animal world. Black Sheep, Bo-Peep and Boy Blue – Mrs Chandos can conjure them up as nobody else that I know.'

'You only say that,' said Jenny, 'because I talk to them. They can't understand the words, but their wonderful instinct tells them all I mean. And they love being talked to, you know. All animals do. Just look at Adamant.'

'My sweet,' said Mansel, 'the communion you held with Adamant shortened my life.'

'And who,' said Falcon, 'is Adamant?'

'I'll tell you one day,' said Mansel. 'I don't know that you'll believe me, but I can

150

always try.'

And so it was after dinner that Falcon took up his tale.

'I drove straight to the Yard, of course. There I reported in person and had a long talk. Feeling all over the country is running high. The Home Office has asked to be kept informed. The AC used these words. "The reputation of the Yard is at stake as never before. High and low are demanding vengeance. We've simply got to get home." I'd told him I was staying with you, and he said he was very glad. When I said Colonel Mansel was here he told me to "rope him in". When I said I was trying to spare the Sisterhood, "That's quite right," he said: "but don't forget – Justice comes first. If they hold out on you, they've got to be racked. I'm very sorry, but Sanctuary's out of date." He quite agreed that the finding of the poison should be announced on Monday. We framed the announcement together, before I left. Finally, he spoke very kindly. "I'll back you, Falcon, in any action you take. This case may call for some sudden, desperate decision at any time. Take it, and God be with you. I certainly shall. I don't care what it costs – we've got to get home."

'Then I went through the stuff on my table.

'Paterson's record was normal. "A good, conscientious GP. Might well have been a consultant in Harley Street. Assistant to Dr

151

– who, on being asked, recommended him to the Home."

'Berryman – not a good chit. Very much what Dallas told me. Subversive of law and order, but disappears if he sees a plain-clothes man. Where there's a strike, he'll be in the nearest pub, standing drinks and doing his stuff. Lives with a doting mother in Grosvenor Square. The servants hate his guts.

'Madame de Porphyry is not staying at The Savoy. She arrived there ten days ago; but when they saw who it was, they said they hadn't a room. She is Madame la Duchesse de Vairie, notorious even in France. The Duke won't divorce her, because he's a very strict Catholic. She's taken a service flat in – House. Keeps very irregular hours. No evidence yet that she ever drives a grey car. But that's being followed up. Involved two years ago in a very unsavoury case. The wife of one of her lovers committed suicide. A good many people thought that it wasn't suicide…

'Then I went back to my flat, had some dinner sent up, thought things over for a while and went to bed.

'At nine o'clock the next morning I took the Great West Road.

'Curfew Place is attractive. The house is not too big – I should say about this size. A pleasant, sheltered garden, bright with flowers. The rest is stabling and paddocks, all in the finest order you ever saw.

'George Selden received me – a man of few words. I think we all know the type – a steady, unemotional soldier, whom nothing will ever shake. Perfectly groomed; a well-worn country suit that had come out of Savile Row – a concession to Sunday, I guessed, and I was right; beautifully polished shoes.

'He took me into a pleasant morning-room.

'As we sat down–

'"Your room's all ready," he said. "I hope you'll eat with me. Anything I can do, you've only to say the word."

'"I'm sure of that. I'd like to see my man and the lawyer's clerk. And then, if it's right by you, we could have a talk."

'Selden opened the door and shouted, *"James"*.

'The butler appeared.

'"Tell those two to come here. The Superintendent wants them." Selden turned to me. "I'm going to see a mare. She's near her time. Tell James when you're ready for me. He'll ring the bell."

'With that, he was gone.

'I couldn't help liking the man. Though he'd never mentioned his loss, I could see it had hit him hard. His fine, grey eyes were dull. Life seemed to have lost its savour. His stable-companion was dead.

'The lawyer's clerk had little enough to say.

'"I've sealed his lordship's desk, sir. That's

in the study, that is. There's only one drawer locked. I expect you've got the key. But I haven't touched anything. There's a safe in the office and quite a number of files. But they're all to do with the horses, and as Major Selden needs them, I let them be.'

'"Quite right."

'"And Mr Fenton asked me to tell you, sir, that if you'd like to see him, I've only to ring him up."

'"Thank you. I'll let you know."

'He left the room, and Welcome gave me his written report.

'There was no meat for me in this, but he hadn't wasted his time. He'd seen all the principal servants within and without. They were broken-hearted. All of them worshipped St Amant. Visitors mostly on Sundays. Luncheon and tea. Sometimes neighbours to dine. But only when St Amant was there. Major Selden 'lived very quiet'. St Amant was often away for two or three nights – very often at Newmarket, where he stayed at The Jockey Club Rooms. Whenever he stayed in London, he used The Savoy. His body-servant, Bolton, went with him everywhere. When he heard the news, he wanted to rush to the Home: but Major Selden told him that, if he did, he'd have him put under arrest. 'How d'you think I feel? But it's not our job.' Feeling among the lads was running high. 'Them –

nuns... Nice sort of nursing home... More like a slaughter-house...' They're counting on you to avenge his lordship's death.

'Welcome had little to add.

'"I think you should see Bolton, sir. He'll hardly talk to me."

'"All right."

'Then I sent him off to find James and ask him to ring the bell. (This hangs in a miniature belfry, built on to the back of the house. On a still day, you can hear it up on the gallops.) Five minutes later, Selden came tramping in.

'"This room all right, Superintendent?"

'"As long as no one can hear."

'"I'll see to that." He let out a bellow. '*James.*'

'The butler appeared.

'"Send Bolton here and bring us something to drink."

'Beer was served – in two of the finest tankards I've ever seen. William the Third, I should say. And Selden lighted a pipe. Then Bolton appeared.

'"Stand to the door, Bolton. And knock if anyone comes."

'"Very good, sir."

'As the door closed–

'"Body-servant," said Selden. "Been with Jo since the war. Out for blood, poor fellow. I feel the same."

'"I don't blame you," I said. "I feel that

way myself. And now tell me this, Major Selden. Did anyone know Lord St Amant better than you?"

"'Nobody knew him as well. I came to live with him in '46. Good enough for me. From that day to this, I've never slept out of my bed."

"'When did you meet him first?"

"'Pulled his ears at Eton in '32."

"'And after that?"

"'Hunting with the Cottesmore. His people lived in the country. I dined at his home once or twice. Really got to know him during the war. Both on the same special duty in 1942. We mucked in together well. I think we fixed things up in '44. DV, of course. He'd got his eye on this place. And then it came off."

"'With everyone else, I suppose, you'd believed him dead."

"'I went to the Memorial Service."

"'Did you indeed? And then he rose from the dead?"

"'You've said it, Superintendent. He'd never talk about it. I think he felt he was to blame for not getting word through. Never dreamed he hadn't been posted as missing. But, if he had, what could he do? He was on his back for three months in the attic of a French farm. Blown up, you know. When he got to the Pyrenees, the snow was down. He got over at last, and the Spaniards picked him up. He broke out of jail and made his way back into France. Then he swam the Bidassoa – he'd had enough of the hills. And then he made Portugal. He never told me all that – I got it from our MA after the war."

"'What a wonderful show. Pity he took it like that."

'Selden shook his head and relighted his pipe.

"'Well, now let's come to this business down at the Home. Poison's been hinted at. That has now been proved. And it wasn't an accident. Had he any enemies?"

"'Looks as though he had one: it's news to me. You couldn't help liking Jo."

"'Women?"

"'All they wanted to do was to put their arms round his neck. But he never went far with them. He'd never have got tied up. Same as me, you know – a bachelor born and bred."

"'Did he ever go to Paris?"

"'From time to time. *Grand Prix,* you know."

"'Did he ever mention a Madame de Porphyry?"

"'Not to me."

"'*Alias La Duchesse de Vairie.*"

"'That's better. She came here once – I forget who brought her along. Made a dead set at Jo, for all to see. Takes a lot to embarrass me, but... Talked French to him all the time, and all the rest of us English. He answered in English, of course, but it didn't do any good. When we sat down to luncheon, Jo put her up my end, though she should have been on his right. By God, was she wild? But he couldn't do anything else. At least he saved the party, more or less."

'"No cause to love him, then?"'

'Selden looked at me.

'"Don't tell me she's taken the veil?"'

'"Good God, no," said I. "But she came to the Home last Sunday and blundered into his room."

'"The devil she did. D'you think…"'

'I shrugged my shoulders.

'"She's down on my list," I said. "No more than that. Tell me this, Major Selden. Does the name of Berryman mean anything to you?"'

'"Old 'Topsy' Berryman's brat. He's got a nuisance value, but nothing more. Not guts enough to be an enemy."

'"A nuisance value. What do you mean by that?"'

'"Well, he's known Jo all his life, because their fathers were friends: but he's fouled his nest for years and nobody speaks to the man: but if he thinks it's safe, he'll speak to you. Well, that's not done, you know. He came up to Jack Benham once: Jack told him then and there that if ever he did it again, he'd give him in charge. But Jo was always so gentle. And so he presumed. Give you a case in point. Jo had been up for the day – to London, I mean. Halfway through dinner that evening he starts to laugh. 'I forgot to tell you, George, I had a show-down today.' 'Who with?' I said. 'Berryman.' 'What's he done now?' said I. 'I found him waiting at White's. He'd told the porter that he was to be my guest.' 'Good God,' said I. 'I hope you warned him off for good and all.' 'I said I was sorry I couldn't ask him to lunch. I may say he was simply filthy: unshaved, no collar on and looked as if he'd slept in his clothes. Because you're a snob, says he. No, said I. But because, if I did, I should certainly have to resign. Then I called a servant and told him to show him out.' What d'you think of that, Superintendent?"

'"Words fail me" said I. "But that's beside the point. Berryman was also a patient down at the Home. Next door but one."

'"God give me strength."

'"He's down on the list, too. A bit higher up now."

'"Poison," said Selden. "He might have the guts for that. But he must have thought himself safe." He shook his head. "I'd put the lady first."

'"Major Selden, I want you to think. You said 'No enemies' – and I have produced to you two. Potential ones, of course. Can't you think of anyone else?"

'"Sorry, Superintendent. My mind was running on racing. Easy enough to make an enemy there. But Jo never did. And now let me think."

'We sat in silence for, I'd say, two minutes at least.

'Then Selden shook his head.

'"God forgive me," he said, "I can't think of anyone else."

'"No dismissed servant?"

'"Oh, no."

'"D'you think he was open with you?"

'"That's my belief."

'"Ever seen him depressed?"

'"Never. He didn't know what it meant."

'"Knocks?"

'"Sometimes. He always took 'em with a smile. There was no one like him, Superintendent. Model yourself on Jo, and you couldn't go wrong."

'I took the keys from my pocket.

'"Can you identify these?"

'Selden picked them up. There were only six.

'"Writing-table, safe – I've got a duplicate – dispatch-case, latch-key – not that he needed that: there was always somebody up. Now what's that? Oh, I know. Roll-top table in the office: but that is never locked. I don't know that one, Superintendent."

'He was holding up the biggest of all.

'"I think," I said, "that that's the key of a

wall-safe." I looked at the makers' name. "Yes, they make safes. I think I'm probably right."

'Selden stared.

'"I never knew he'd got one."

'"They're very small safes, you know. All right for jewellery."

'"He'd very little of that, and he never locked it up."

'"It's probably here somewhere – behind a picture, perhaps."

'"We'll have a look. No, wait a minute. *Bolton.*"

'The valet entered the room.

'"Tell James to come here."

'When the butler arrived–

'"The Superintendent says he thinks there's a wall-safe here."

'"A wall-safe, sir?"

'I took up the running.

'"You may not have seen one, James. All that shows is a little door in the wall. About a foot square. They're often behind a picture."

'"I've never seen one here, sir. And once a year we have all the pictures down."

'"All right," said Selden.

'The butler withdrew.

'"We might try Bolton," I said.

'"Why not? *Bolton.*"

'The valet re-entered the room.

'"D'you know of a wall-safe here?"

'The valet hesitated. Then–

'"I don't think his lordship would like—"
'Selden burst out.
'"Don't be a fool. The Superintendent's trying to get at the truth. He's got to see everything. Don't you want this bloody murderer put to death?"
'The valet crumpled.
'"I'm sorry, sir. But I don't think anyone knew it, except his lordship and me."
'"Where is it, Bolton?" I said.
'"In his lordship's bedroom, sir."
'"Come on," said Selden, rising.
'The valet led us upstairs to a very pleasant chamber upon the first floor. Then he opened a built-in wardrobe – a hanging wardrobe, this. It was full of suits. He took out three of the hangers and pushed the rest to one side.
'"You'll see it there in the wall, sir."
'Selden put in his head and looked to the left.
'"That'll be it," he said. "All right, Bolton. You go and stand to the door."
'The valet withdrew.
'I tried the key and the wall-safe opened at once.
'There was very little inside. I took the contents out and put them in Selden's hands. A fine, gold pocket-watch, attached to a cable chain. A magnificent diamond ring. A foolscap envelope, sealed. And that was all.
'Selden crossed to the bed and laid them down.

'"That's his father's watch," he said. "I remember the chain. And that's a ring of his mother's – at least, I think it is. And that's his handwriting."

'On the envelope was written, *To be burned, unopened, in the event of my death.*

'"I'm sorry," I said, "but I'll have to open that. You never know, Major Selden."

'Selden thought for a moment. Then–

'"You're right," he said. "But if it doesn't help, you'll burn it at once."

'"Indeed, I will. And I think we might keep it to ourselves. I'll give you a receipt, if you like."

'"Not on your life. I haven't seen the thing."

'"But you do understand, Major Selden?"

'Selden looked at me.

'"Look here, Superintendent. All my hope is in you. Somebody did Jo in – the finest gentleman in England, and my familiar friend. If you could show me the –, he'd never get as far as the gallows. He'd never come to be tried. You'd never get me off him, until he was dead."

'"Now I know where I am," I said. "And now I'll be very frank. I'm doing my level best. But it's a hell of a case. And I must have everyone's help. I know I can count on yours. But Bolton may know something which he feels he should keep to himself. You might have a word with him, and tell him that I shan't talk."

"'By God, I will. D'you want to see him now?'"

"'After luncheon, please. First James and then him. And now have a look at this." I took out St Amant's wrist-watch. "D'you know how he came by that?'"

"'I've no idea. Had it as long as I've known him. New straps, of course.'"

"'During the war?'"

"'I rather think so. I can't be sure of that.'"

'I put it back in my pocket.

"'Well, don't forget I've got it, if anyone asks. I've his notecase and cheque-book, too. And, by the way, his suitcase is in my car. I don't want to upset poor Bolton, so I'll have it put in the hall. Oh, one thing more. This is his ring." Selden looked and nodded. "I think we might put it in the wall-safe.'"

"'Good idea.'"

'I put the envelope into my pocket. The watch and chain and the rings, I put into the safe. Then I locked this up.

"'Bolton might put the clothes back.'"

"'I'll tell him to.'"

'I glanced at my watch.

"'What time d'you lunch, Major Selden?'"

"'About one o'clock.'"

"'Then I think I'll go through his desk.'"

"'You won't want me for that.'"

"'No. But I'd like the lawyer's clerk. I'll put aside any papers on which I want your advice.'"

'"Right. Anything you want, call James."

'"I may want to speak to the Yard."

'"He'll get you through."

'He showed me the way to the study and sent for the clerk.

'The study was really a miniature library. Luxurious, leather armchairs on either side of the hearth. A leather sofa to match. A pedestal-table. Shoulder-high bookcases full of sporting books – an original edition of Surtees, Beckford's *Thoughts on Hunting* and other famous works. A number of well-known novels stood in a case by themselves. On the walls above the cases, a number of sporting prints.

'There was nothing in the papers that I could see. The locked drawer held personal letters, all to do with horses and racing, many from well-known men. One note was signed with a very well-known name. *Dear Lord St Amant. It was more than kind of you to write as you did. I must confess that I, too, believed that my horse had won: but nobody can dispute what the camera says. (I sometimes wonder how many wrong decisions have been given in the years that are past.) And pray don't think that I feel badly about the result. I might have, if the race had not gone to you: but, if I am to be beaten, I would sooner lose to you than to any man that I know. Yours very sincerely, –.* Another was signed with another well-known name. *My lord, I'm properly upset about this afternoon. I wouldn't mind so much, if I hadn't been riding for you. I don't think it was my fault, but I can't bear letting you down. Yours respectfully –.* Pencilled on this was a note in St Amant's hand. *Dear–. You are not to reproach yourself. You rode a beautiful race: but the filly wasn't quite good enough. Yours. St A.'*

Falcon paused there and looked round.

'I particularly noted those letters, because I think they show how justly beloved and respected the dead man was.'

'They seem to me,' said Mansel, 'to emphasize two things. The first is that such a man's enemies must have been very few: the second is that the man who murdered St Amant must have been bold indeed.'

'Or round the bend,' said I.

There was a moment's silence. Then Falcon went on.

'I locked up the drawer again, gave the bunch of keys to the clerk and bade him make out a receipt. While he was doing that–

'"That's the key of a wall-safe," I said. "The valet will show the executors where it is."

'It was half past twelve by then, so I left the house for a stroll. Selden was just coming in, so he offered to show me round.

'To one who knows nothing of horses, it's still a showplace. Coach-houses all one side of the stable-yard by the house. The doors were wide open, so I could see the cars. Two Rolls – the smaller model – one black and one grey; two station-wagons, three horse-boxes and two trucks; all of them polished and shining and looking as good as new.

'I pointed to the Rolls.

'"His cars?"

'"Yes. I had the use of them – if I wanted to go to London or a meeting or something like that."

'"Chauffeurs?"

'"Two regular ones. Do nothing else, I mean. And Bolton can drive. I never drive myself, but Jo very often did. Not always, you know."

'"When were they used last?"

'"The Rolls? Not since he went away. He drove himself to the Home and Bolton brought the car back."

'Here a third station-wagon pulled into the yard.

'"First chauffeur," said Selden.

'"I thought it was Bolton," I said.

'"Twin brother. We call him Fred."

'"Keys of the cars?"

'"In his charge."

'We left the stable-yard and came to the stables proper, further on. There wasn't time to see much. Loose-box after loose-box, name after name. Sick bay, farrier's shop, home paddocks and the rest. Of course I was out of my depth, but really racehorses are the most lovely things. Then we went back to the house.

'A simple, English luncheon, beautifully cooked and served.

'After luncheon, I sent for Welcome and told him I'd take him to London the following day. Gave him the afternoon off, to do as he pleased. Then I thought things over and made some notes. Selden, I think, was dozing – a habit, perhaps, of his on a Sunday afternoon.

'At three I saw the butler – an excellent type of servant, very precise.

'"A sad business this, James."

'"Most shocking, sir. For us that lived with his lordship, it seems like some dreadful dream. I shall never forget when the Major broke the news. He was so much upset that he couldn't speak the words. So he took a pencil and paper and wrote them down. Excuse me, sir." He took a case from his pocket, and drew out a sheet of notepaper, folded in four. "That's what he gave me, sir."

'The writing was very shaky.

'*His lordship found dead this morning. They seem to suspect foul play. Anyway Scotland Yard has been called in. Better tell the others – they've got to know.*

'I handed it back.

'"I'm very sorry for him."

'"He's taking it very hard, sir. But so are we all."

'"I've no doubt of that. I'm taking it hard myself. Who d'you think did it, James?" The butler stared. "You're thinking that that's the question which you should be asking me. Well, I hope to be able to tell you before very long. But just now I want your guess."

"'Well, sir, since you ask me, I'll tell you I'm properly beat. I've been over the last eight years, for I came to Curfew Place in 1946. I've thought of all the people that's come and gone. But I can't think of one that might have wished him ill. High and low, sir, they liked and respected his lordship – as well they might."

"'Were you ever told that if somebody came to the house, he was to be sent away?'"

"'Never once, sir.'"

"'Did his lordship ever say that if so-and-so rang up, you were to say he was out?'"

"'Never, sir. He'd never speak, if he could help it. I'd bring him the message and take another one back.'"

"'You got to know the technique.'"

"'Precisely, sir. Some calls I knew he would wish to deal with himself.'"

"'Very well. I'm afraid poor Bolton is very much upset.'"

"'He's beside himself, sir. He was so close to his lordship – went with him everywhere. He couldn't bear his lordship being away at the Home. Out of his charge, you see. He wanted to stay in the village, but his lord-ship wouldn't have that. And now he seems to feel that it would never have happened if he'd been there."

"'Poor fellow," I said. "Well, James, I'm much obliged. Don't think you haven't helped me, because you have. Get hold of Bolton, will you? I'd like to see him now."

"'Certainly, sir."

Two minutes later the valet entered the room.

'I looked him full in the eyes.

"'Now, Bolton, you've got to help me. I'm doing my very best to help all of you. I can't bring his lordship back, but I think we shall all feel better, if I can bring this crime home."

"'That's very true, sir."

"'When his lordship went to the Home, you drove him there."

"'No, sir. He drove the car there, and I brought it back."

"'I see. Did you know the way?"

"'No, sir. Nor did his lordship. But it was easy to find."

"'You made for Ne'er-do-well?"

"'Yes, sir. And there I asked."

"'If you'd known where it was, you needn't have gone through the village."

"'That is so, sir. We had to come back to cross roads, two miles off."

"'That's the way you drove back?"

"'Yes, sir."

"'Now this is very important. Did you take your brother with you when you drove there on Monday night?"

'The man recoiled, and a hand went up to his mouth.

'"It's quite all right," I said. "I only want to know if you went alone."

'The poor man's eyes were starting.

'"It – it was Monday night. Not Tuesday."

'"I know it was Monday," I said. "Did you go alone?"

'"I went alone, sir," said Bolton. "My brother gave me the keys."

'"You took the grey Rolls."

'"Yes, sir."

'"And parked her a little way off."

'"Yes, sir."

'"And then walked back."

'"Yes, sir."

'"Did you enter the grounds?"

'"No, sir. It was easy enough to get in, but I thought there might be a watchman, and so I stayed outside."

'"Did you know where his lordship was lodged?"

'"Not for certain, sir. But we saw the terrace, as we come up to the Home. And his lordship said, I'd like a room on that terrace. I hope they give me one. And somehow I thought they would."

'"What time did you get there, Bolton?"

'"To the Home itself, sir?"

'"Yes."

'"It must have been just about eleven o'clock."

"'Did you see any lights? In the rooms on the terrace, I mean.'"

"'One room was lighted, sir. But only just. A table lamp, I should say.'"

"'Could you say which room it was?'"

"'I'd say it was near the middle. I can't be sure.'"

"'You wondered if it was his?'"

"'Yes, sir.'"

"'Did you see the light of a torch?'"

"'I can't say I did, sir. But this was Monday night, sir.'"

"'I know. Did you see the light go out – the light in the room, I mean?'"

"'Yes, sir. It must have been half past eleven. So then I went back to the car.'"

"'You're sure you saw nothing else?'"

"'I saw a flicker, sir, just as I was turning to go. But it wasn't a torch. I don't know what it was.'"

"'What d'you mean by a flicker?'"

"'A very faint light indeed. It seemed to be higher somehow.'"

"'Did it come and go?'"

"'It stayed for a moment or two: and then it went out.'"

"'You'd put that at half past eleven?'"

"'Thereabouts, sir. When I got back to the car, the clock said twenty to twelve.'"

"'Did you go to the Home more than once?'"

"'Twice, sir. The first time on Friday.'"

172

"'Why did you go, Bolton?'"

'The poor man's look made me think of a beaten dog.

"'I know I shouldn't have done it: but I couldn't bear, sir, him lying sick without me.'"

"'I quite understand, Bolton. It made things better if you could be close to him.'"

"'That's right, sir. I wanted to stay in the village, but his lordship said no.' Then he burst out. "If only I'd gone on Tuesday…'"

"'It wouldn't have made any difference. Take that from me. And now let's look back. You always accompanied his lordship, if ever he stayed away.'"

"'Always, sir, if he went away for the night.'"

"'Recall anyone who wasn't friendly to him?'"

"'Not a single soul, sir, in all these years.'"

"'Did you answer the telephone?'"

"'Very often, sir. Always at The Savoy.'"

"'Did he ever say, Tell them I'm out?'"

"'I never remember that, sir. He'd say, Say I'm engaged and ask them to leave a message. He was very patient, sir. Especially with the Press. And the things he used to do, sir, that nobody knew. Time and again, I've followed him down The Embankment late at night. Talking to down-and-outs and giving them the price of a meal. I've seen him sit down beside them and lay his hand on their arm. Of course he never knew I was there. They'll miss him, they will: but no one will miss him like me."

'It was really very moving to see such genuine love…

'Later on, I walked to the stables alone. Two or three lads in a doorway were handling hay. As I went by–

'"The stable's on you, sir," said one.

'"That's right," said another. "God knows you can't bring him back, but show us the – that did it. That's all we ask."

'"You can't want it more than I do. Once let me get on his heels and I'll never let go."

'"That's the stuff, sir."

'"No guilty, but insane, sir."

'"Not if I can help it," I said.

'And as I passed on–

'"Good luck, sir … good luck … good luck."

'Then an old fellow came up and took off his shabby cap.

'"I taught his lordship to ride, sir. It don't seem so long ago. An' now – I can't 'ardly believe it. Always so gay and gallant and full of life. My son's first farrier here. When he reads they've sent for you, It's all right, Dad, he says, Superintendent Falcon'll get the – down. An' you will, won't you, sir?"

'"I give you my word," I said, "I'll do my best."

'He shook my hand, with the tears running down his face…

'After dinner we sat in the study, and

Selden talked quite a lot. All about St Amant, of course. Just what I wanted, you know. I got a very clear portrait.'

'Outlook,' said Mansel, smiling.

'That's right. The victim's outlook is often just as important as that of anyone else.'

'I'm sure poor Selden was only too thankful to talk.'

'I think he was. He seemed distressed when I said I must go the next morning. But to stay on there would have been a waste of time. And even if I had had to come back, I should have gone away. Day of the funeral, you see. When I said goodbye the next morning, Selden thanked me for coming and asked me to come again. "When it's all over, you know. No shop. But you're easy to talk to. Done me a lot of good. I'll give you a hack and we'll have a look at the gallops."

'"That's an engagement," I said.

'"Good man."

Falcon raised his eyebrows and pushed back his hair. 'I think I must go one day. I'm so desperately sorry for Selden. He's broken up.' He sighed. 'So much, then, for my visit to Curfew Place.'

'It was very quick of you, Falcon, to see the answer to the riddle set by the waiting car.'

'Oh, I don't know. The moment I saw the grey Rolls, I wondered if that was the car the cyclist had seen. And then it occurred to me that surreptitiously to visit the Home was exactly what a devoted servant would do. The thing was to get Bolton to admit it.'

'A most accomplished proceeding from first to last. As a result, Madame la Duchesse de Vairie has fallen right back.'

'Yes. She's still in the running, of course. And she could have had the poison. I'm not losing sight of her. If she should book for France, they'll get on the telephone.

'On Monday afternoon I rang up Berrymans' home. After a little while he came to the telephone.

'"Mr Berryman?"

'"Yes."

'"Head sleuth, here. I'd like another talk. Will you come to me? Or shall I come to you?"

'"When?"

'"Half an hour from now."

'"Where are you?"

'"In my room at Scotland Yard."

'"I don't care which."

'"Very well, then. You come to me."

'He hesitated. Then–

'"All right."

'Thirty-five minutes later, they brought him up to my room.

'He threw himself into a chair and took out a pipe.

'"What d'you want me for?" he said.

'"I told you," I said, "I wanted another talk."

""–well stuck, I suppose."

""You can suppose what you please. Why didn't you tell me you knew Lord St Amant quite well?"

'I saw his muscles contract. After an obvious struggle–

""You didn't ask me, for one thing."

""I see. And for another?"

""Whether I knew him or not was nothing to do with you."

""I don't think that's the answer," I said.

""What d'you mean?"

""What I say. I think the true answer is that you didn't want me to know."

""Why?"

""Because, if I'd known that you knew him, you wouldn't have dared to say that you didn't know he was there."

""What are you getting at?"

""The truth, I hope this time. In a case like this, Mr Berryman, *suppressio veri* makes a detective think. How did Lord St Amant know you were there?"

'The man started violently. Then–

""Who says he did?"

""He told another patient he'd seen you … as he walked past your room. D'you still maintain that you didn't know he was there?"

""How should I know he was a patient? Patients don't walk about."

""Some patients can – but prefer to lie in bed."

'The man went very white.

'"Are you ... suggesting..."

'"I'm suggesting nothing," I said. "Are you a member of White's?"

'Berryman began to tremble.

'"Oh, my God," he whimpered.

'"*One lord the less*, Mr Berryman?"

'Breathing most hard–

'"You can't hold that against me," he panted, "I – I only said that in jest."

'"Some people might find such a sense of humour strange. I mean, they might even think that such a brutal remark argued a brutal mind."

'The man went to pieces.

'"Oh, God, why did I say it? Oh, God, be kind. You know I never did it. I've never had any poison in all my life. I never knew where his room was. I never set foot on the terrace while I was there."

"Easy to say these things."

'"But they're true,' he screamed. "They're true. And – and I couldn't do a murder ... I'd – be afraid."

'I sat and looked at the creature, thinking of his activities down in the docks and then of St Amant walking along the Embankment, comforting down-and-outs.

'"Well, that'll do for the moment. You're going to Brighton, aren't you?"

'"Oh, God, I'm being watched."

'Such abject fear is a very unpleasant sight.

'"There's a man outside the door. He'll show you out."

'Berryman got to his feet and wiped his face.

'"If you w – want me again," he stammered.

'"You'll be informed."

'Berryman went.'

'I can't help feeling,' said Mansel, 'that you enjoyed yourself.'

'Thoroughly,' said Falcon. 'It did me a lot of good to reduce the sweep. He's out, of course. When he said he'd be afraid to do murder, that was the honest truth. Those words came straight from what we must call his heart. An altogether contemptible piece of work.'

'How wanton,' I said, 'Fortune can sometimes be. She pushes Berryman on you, as a card-sharper pushes a card. Inclination, opportunity, motive – he had them all. Dallas, Paterson, Selden volunteer deadly evidence. You could have had a warrant whenever you pleased.'

'Without a doubt,' said Falcon. 'I don't say that he would have gone down; but he would have been committed for trial.'

'The pace-maker cracks,' said Mansel.

'Exactly,' said Falcon. 'I know that he never did it. I've got to look somewhere else.

'I haven't much more to tell you, although my days were full. I suppose you'd call it routine, but it can be more than that. You

179

must do some things yourself. You know what it is. If you've got to be perfectly sure that something's been perfectly done, the only thing to do is to do it yourself.'

'You're telling us,' said Mansel. 'And in a case like this...'

'That is the truth. In this particular case, I have so little to go on that every scrap of information must go into the sieve.'

Mansel drew in his breath.

'Falcon,' he said, 'I'm perfectly sure you'll get home, but what a hell of a case.'

'Yes,' said Falcon, 'it is. It's quite the most difficult problem I've ever been set. Hardly a pointer – except to Will-o'-the-Wisps. But it's been a help to be away from the scene. Sometimes one's focus is better, when one is not on the spot. It's like standing back from a picture. Things seem to fall into perspective...'

'That, I can understand. Inquest resumed on Friday?'

'Yes. That can't be helped. The Coroner must have his show. Proof that poison was found. I saw Sir William: he's coming down himself. And then another adjournment.'

Mansel smiled.

'You've blessed a good many Inquests.'

'That's very true. But this one is not going to help. It only interferes with my job.'

'Your brain,' said Jenny, 'must get so terribly tired. I mean you never stop thinking.'

'I know. One becomes obsessed. That's

180

why it helps me so much to stay with you.'

'We don't seem to give you much rest.'

'That's of choice. As I've said before, it helps me no end to make an informal report. But at dinner, for instance, I quite forgot the case. By the way, you were speaking of the Brevets. And when I asked who they were, you, all of you, laughed and promised to tell me one day.'

'It's not a short story,' I said.

'I'd like to hear it – now.'

'Go on, William,' said Mansel.

'Daniel Gedge,' I said. 'I expect you know his name.'

'The infamous Auntie Emma. He took care to keep out of England: but, if half what I've heard is true, he had a handsome run.' He hesitated. 'I did hear it whispered that you had seen him off.'

'William did that,' said Mansel. 'He stole my show. But he couldn't help himself, for the man was out to kill.'

'According to my information, he often was.'

'He was that night,' I said.

'Well, Brevet was his confederate ... and some words which Brevet used, when he was awaiting the order to put me to death, betrayed an outlook which some people share today. We speak of them as "The Brevets". I put it in *Red in the Morning*. He told me he hated me – not for what I had done, but for what I was. "I am a criminal, and you are a country squire. Do you wonder that I hate you, Chandos? Do you wonder that I look forward to spilling what brains you have?" Of course, he'd never have said it, if he'd dreamed I was going to live. And now you shall have the context.'

Cut it short as I would, the tale took time to tell. But Falcon listened intently to every word, sometimes asking questions and smiling when I came to Mona Lelong.

'You beat us there,' he said.

'Only just.'

'She was on the *Harvest Moon*.'

I nodded.

'You came in too late, Superintendent.'

'Goalby wasn't up to your weight. When he told me you'd changed a wheel, I nearly died. "But I saw the flat tire," he said. "My God," I said, "what d'you take Mr Chandos for?"'

Mansel was shaking with laughter.

'A nice reputation, William, we've got at the Yard.'

Falcon looked at Jenny.

'Mine is big, Mrs Chandos. But theirs is fabulous. And now please go on, Mr Chandos.'

When I had done—

'What a desperate business,' said Falcon. 'Of course Gedge was out of the jungle – a terribly dangerous man. It was he who killed Lafère, the best policeman the French had got. Lafère had sworn to get him. Somebody told Gedge – and that was that. They gave up trying then, and Gedge used to do as he pleased. But I'd never heard of Brevet. My word, what a combination! You deserve the Legion of Honour for putting them down. But you're right. There are plenty of Brevets knocking about today. When you're tired of that name, you can call them "the wilful failures".' He sat back and covered his eyes. 'There you are, you see. You've done the trick. I haven't thought of my business for nearly an hour.'

'Good,' said Jenny. 'Now that we know, we'll have to do it again.'

But we never did.

The following day, Thursday, was very hot.

On the terrace, after luncheon–

'Falcon,' I said, 'is *distrait.*'

Mansel looked up.

'I think so, too. That means he's on to something. He told us all about Curfew, but he said very little about what he did in London, when he got back.'

'Only the Berryman interview.'

'And he was there for two days.'

'Two and a half,' said Jenny. 'Perhaps what was in the envelope gave him a clue.'

'I think you're right, my darling. He could hardly divulge its contents, even to us; and they, no doubt, commanded all he was doing in London during the next two days.'

'I think,' said Mansel, 'that, when the scent grows hot, Falcon is going to dry up. Not that he doesn't trust us, but he no longer needs the relief of opening his heart. Instead, he requires the silence which high concentration must have.'

'A case like this,' said I, 'must impose a tremendous strain. Look at the feeling St Amant's death has aroused. High and low are demanding his murderer's head. And Falcon alone can produce it. No one can help him: even Rogers admits that he's out of his depth. So far as we know, he has next to nothing to go on: and the nuns, in whose home the murder was done, are reluctant to talk. And they can't be grilled, because they mean no wrong. Look at Sister Josephine.'

'William,' said Mansel, 'I couldn't agree with you more. And just look at the poison – Mafra. Talk about narrowing the field. Who's ever heard of Mafra? Even the Press hasn't got it – I mean, what Sir William says. Virtually unknown in England. Known to the police in France. Sources of supply, undiscoverable. Poison is never easy, but arsenic gives you a chance. But Mafra – no. Of course it made us stare at Madame de Porphyry: and in view of what Selden said, she probably nursed a grudge. But how did she know that St Amant was taking tablets? Anyway Falcon seems to have written her off.

Oh, no. As I said last night, it is a hell of a case. Still, Falcon's terribly good. He makes a lot of our exploits. Compared with this, they were very showy stuff. Our art was that of the blacksmith, and I am by no means ashamed of the iron we wrought. But this is work for a goldsmith, requiring infinite patience and very high skill.'

When Falcon returned that evening and said that, by our leave, he would have to go out after dinner and so would not talk that night, we did not know what to think: but, when he came in on Friday, looking most pale and drawn, and asked if we might have some music, when dinner was over and done, I think we all felt that a crisis of sorts was at hand.

Beethoven, Chopin, Bach – one after another, famous orchestras rendered their deathless works; and Falcon sat there listening, with his eyes on the slow wood fire.

As the last of the records faded, he got to his feet. Then he turned to Jenny and took her hand in both his.

'You're very sweet, Mrs Chandos, to bear with so trying a guest. And now, if you will forgive me, I'm going directly to bed.'

'Sleep well,' said Jenny gently. 'Bell has taken some barley-water up to your room.'

Falcon held her hand tight. Then he released it and turned to Mansel and me.

'Good night,' he said, smiling. 'I've much

to be thankful for.'

As the door closed behind him–

'Oh, dear,' said Jenny.

I put my arm about her and held her close.

'Cold blood, my sweet. That's the trouble. Jonathan and I could never have done what we did in cold blood. But a policeman isn't so lucky. And Falcon is like a racehorse – a very sensitive man.'

'William is right,' said Mansel. 'He nearly always is. And now,' he added quietly, 'I think we should go to bed, too.'

At half past two the next day I was crossing the hall, when I heard the crunch of gravel which told me a car was at hand. The front door was open, and so I stood where I was.

Falcon.

He spoke to his driver shortly. Then he mounted the steps and entered the house.

The man looked pale and drawn, as he had the night before: but he was very calm.

As the service door was opened–

'Where's Mrs Chandos?' he said.

In some surprise–

'She's out with Bell,' I said. 'She won't be back before four.'

'Then that's all right.'

'Have you lunched?' said I.

'No, but I haven't time. I've got to leave for London in half an hour.'

'Sandwiches, Carson,' I said. 'And brandy

and soda at once – in the dining-room. And after that, will you pack the Superintendent's things?'

'Certainly, sir.'

'I'd just like to wash,' said Falcon...

Three minutes later he entered the dining-room.

Mansel was sitting at the table, facing Falcon's chair.

As I poured a brandy and soda–

'All over,' said Falcon. 'I shall be back tomorrow and then I'll tell you all. But if you'd like to hear it, I'll give you the last scene now.'

Carson's knock fell upon the door.

'Come in,' I said.

Carson entered the room with sandwiches on a tray.

'Oh, thank you, Carson,' said Falcon, taking his seat. He looked at me. 'May he see that my driver has something?'

'Of course.'

Carson withdrew.

'Eat and drink first,' I said. 'We're going to talk. We knew, of course, you were coming up to the jump: but though we've both thought a good deal, we haven't said much.'

'Silence is infectious,' said Mansel. 'Oh, and by the way, I'll make you a present of this. This time a week ago I was not at all sure that you'd ever make an arrest. No man can make bricks without straw: and you had

187

no straw.'

'I agree,' said I. 'Looking the facts in the face, the persons who *could* have done it were very few. And most of them were well above suspicion. But what got me down was the poison. I couldn't see how on earth you could bring that home. How could you prove possession of such a drug?'

'Possession – never,' said Mansel. 'But the likelihood of possession – sufficiently strong to satisfy a jury… For me, though I never said so, Sir William's letter very near sounded a knell. It reduced us to the Duchess: and though she seemed to stand out, I had a feeling that it wasn't as easy as that.'

'And then,' said I, 'exactly a week ago, just before you left for London, we thought you seemed rather quiet. And, since neither of us is a fool, that made us think.'

'The trouble was,' said Mansel, 'we didn't know what to think. Unless you had held something back – and I didn't think you had done that – we could not see what had given you cause to fall silent, just at the last.'

Falcon drained his glass. Then he wiped his lips and laid his napkin down.

When I offered him cigarettes, he shook his head.

Then he glanced at his watch and began to talk.

'At eight o'clock last night, the Mother Superior received a letter from me. This is what it said.

Madam,
You will receive me tomorrow precisely at ten o'clock.
Your obedient servant,

Richard Falcon.
Superintendent of the CID.'

Mansel and I sat as though turned to stone.

Falcon proceeded quietly.

'At two minutes to ten this morning, I entered the doors of the Home. Rogers was at my heels. In the second car, the blinds of which were drawn, were sitting two women police. They had come down from London at my request.

'I knocked on the well-known door and entered at once.

'Seated, as usual, at her table, the Mother Superior surveyed me grimly enough.

'"Superintendent," she said, "I am not accustomed—"

'"You are under arrest," I said, "for the murder of Lord St Amant. It is my duty to warn you that anything you say will be taken down and may be used in evidence against you."

'With that, I took out my book...

'The woman never moved, but her eyes were like coals of fire.

189

'Then she burst out.

'"That puling fool Sister Josephine gave you your cue. Until that moment I had you in your place. You thought you were sharing my counsel." She threw back her head and let out a dreadful laugh. "Church and State, you boasted, both are subject to the Law. You thought I accepted that statement – that arrogant blasphemy. To encourage your fool's belief, I attended your puny court and bowed to your Coroner. Let me disillusion you. The State is subject to the laws of man: the Church to the laws of God. You execute the one: I administer the other. As such an administratrix, I put Lord St Amant to death... The world will not forgive me for what I did: but that is nothing to me, for what I did was right. The man had to die. He had the charm of the serpent that commended the apple to Eve. And, but for your blundering foot, all would have been well."

'She drew in her breath.

'Then she picked up an envelope.

'"When they brought me your note last night, I knew what it meant. You'd ferreted out something, behind my back. Perhaps you found the tablet I dropped – close to my private door. I had no desire to be questioned – like Sister Josephine. And so I wrote down this statement, writing far into the night. I need no justification for what I do. This is a statement of fact, and nothing else. Take it and read it and feel ashamed of your manhood – and in future render to God the things that are God's."

'She threw the envelope to me. My eyes were on hers, and I let it fall to the ground.

'"You think you have done your duty: but that is because you're a fool." Her face was working, and she was breathing hard. "I'll tell you what you have done. You have destroyed this House – this precious institution which I have built. For I am the cornerstone: and with my going, the edifice must collapse. And my sheep will have no shepherd. The ship, without its helmsman, will drift upon the rocks. That's my reward for bruising the serpent's head, for doing my bounden duty…"

'"That will do," I said. "What else you have to say can be said in another place." I tapped twice on the door behind me: that was a signal to Rogers to fetch the women police. "I must ask you to come with me. If you wish to arrange yourself first–"

'She threw back her head again and laughed that terrible laugh. That seemed to set her coughing… As she drew out a handkerchief, I stepped forward and caught her wrist.

'She stared at my hand. Then she lifted her eyes to my face.

'"The moment I saw you," she said, "I knew you were dangerous. But there's another sergeant, more strict in his arrest."

191

'Here a knock fell upon the door.

'As I called to Rogers to enter, she seemed to lift herself up and then fell sideways, almost into my arms.

'With the help of the women police I eased her on to the floor.

'Then I spoke to Rogers, whose eyes were half out of his head.

'"Dr Paterson, quick! And Sister Geneviève. Run out and call their names."

'As he ran out of the room, I picked the envelope up and put it away.

'One of the women looked up.

'"I think she's dead, sir."

'I nodded.

'"The doctor will be here in a moment."

'Sister Geneviève was the first to arrive.

'I must say I admire that woman. She just went down on her knees by the Mother Superior's side, peered at her face and then took hold of her wrist. Then she sat back on her heels and put her face in her hands.

'I addressed the women police.

'"Wait outside."

'As they left the room, Paterson arrived at a run.

'"Good God," he said.

'Then he went down on his knees, to feel her heart.

'At a gesture from me, Rogers shut the door.

'"What happened, Superintendent?"

'"She was under arrest," I said. "For the murder of Lord St Amant. She had two tablets of Mafra within her mouth. When I said she must come to the Station, she laughed and swallowed them."

'Sister Geneviève stayed still as she was, but Paterson stared at me, as if I was out of my mind.

'When he spoke, his voice was hoarse.

'"But the thing's incredible."

'"I know it is. But it's true. She admitted committing the murder before she died."

'"God Almighty," said Paterson.

'"I'll tell you later," I said. "I hope you'll do the post-mortem. Rogers, get in touch with the police."

'When Rogers returned, I told him to stay in the room with one of the women police. Then–

'"Sister Geneviève," I said, "it's my duty to search her bedroom. Will you please accompany me?"

'Without a word, she complied. She led the way, and I followed – with one of the women police. It was a most dreadful duty, as you will believe. But I found what I wanted – but never dared hope that I'd find. Two tablets of Mafra, still in their special case.'

Falcon put his hand in his pocket and took out an envelope. He opened it over the table, and something slid out.

This was a thin, oblong, transparent

capsule or case; three quarters of an inch in length, three eighths of an inch in breadth, and, I should say, one thirty-second of an inch thick. Within, we could see two white tablets, lying side by side. That such a case could have laid behind and beside the teeth of the lower jaw, was perfectly clear. I cannot believe that, so bestowed, it would have been noticeable.

'There you are,' said Falcon. 'Sir William wouldn't believe that saliva wouldn't dissolve that special case. But I can swear to that. She had them in her mouth when I entered the room. I prayed that she had, you know. A trial would have been too awful. That's why I let her talk. And then, when nothing happened, I said she must come with me. I had to stop her, of course, when she put her hand to her mouth.'

'You're a scrupulous man,' said Mansel.

'I find if one does one's duty, one usually has one's reward. But I'm not too scrupulous. Her written confession is going to be suppressed. At least, I hope it is. The AC will have to decide.' He glanced again at his watch and got to his feet. 'And now I must go. I hope to be back tomorrow. There's only one thing.' He turned and looked at me. 'The Sisters may have a visitor twice a year. I have reason to think that Sister Helena is in the deepest distress. Would you allow Mrs Chandos – provided, of course, she consents – to go to see her tomorrow? All traces, of course, will be gone.'

'She'll jump at it,' said I. 'I'll take her over myself.'

'In that case, will you send a note to Sister Geneviève? To say that she may expect her at, say, four o'clock?'

'Of course.'

'Very well. I'll write it now.'

The note which he wrote at my table was simple enough.

DEAR SISTER GENEVIÈVE,

The friend of whom I spoke will arrive tomorrow at about four o'clock. Please believe and assure Sister Helena that she will tell me nothing of what transpires. Not one single word.

Yours very sincerely,
RICHARD FALCON.

As I handed it back–

'Now may I write to Mrs Chandos?'

'Of course.'

'I'd rather not show it to you.'

'I'm more than content, Superintendent.'

Falcon wrote a few lines. Then he folded the sheet in two and gave it to me. As I slipped it into my pocket–

'Will you give that to her just before she enters the Home?'

'I promise.'

'Oh, one thing more. You'd better have a

card for the constable at the gates.' He took a card from his case and wrote and initialled four words.

Pass bearer without question.
RF.

Two minutes later Falcon left the house. As his car disappeared–
'Dallas was right,' said Mansel. 'What a man! And she was above suspicion. Not one in a thousand would ever have looked at her. Her exalted position and her commanding presence saw to that. To raise your eyes to her was *lèse majesté*. No one but Falcon would have done it, and no one but Falcon could ever have brought it home. If murder is done in a British Embassy, the one person you do rule out is the Ambassador himself. His great position, his standing forbid any other course... I must confess that it never entered my head.'
'I thought it was Paterson.'
'So did I.'
I drew in my breath.
'But what a fearful ordeal. I'm not surprised that he was all in last night.'
'He must have prayed she'd take poison.'
'Then why,' said I, 'why did he catch her wrist?'
'I think that, when she coughed, he knew it was in her mouth.'

'Out of her mind of course.'

'Say rather fanatic. It comes to much the same thing. Falcon will certainly tell us when he comes back. Apart from anything else, my belief is this. It's perfectly clear that St Amant was a most attractive man. We know he was very handsome and had a remarkable charm. Selden said, "You couldn't help liking Jo." Now the Mother Superior was a nun. She was a gaunt ascetic, who many years ago had subdued the flesh. But such was St Amant's charm that she had to respond to this, against her will. He actually made her laugh... Even to her, he proved irresistible. He had stormed that seemingly impregnable fortress in which was confined her heart. He had set the prisoner leaping. That night she scourged herself. And then she perceived that such a man was a menace, the embodiment of the serpent in human guise. And so she found it her duty to put him to death. You remember how she harped upon duty. She decided that it was her duty to commit this terrible crime.'

'I've no doubt you're right,' said I. 'But Falcon can't read hearts. And if he can, it isn't evidence.'

'Oh, no. There's a lot behind it. But speculation is idle. We'll have to wait for him. But, you know, it's a great achievement. And it's tied up and posted, William – by registered mail. No one can ever dispute it. *A dose of*

Mafra, such as Sir William described, has lain on your dining-room table. And Falcon found that in her room.'

I nodded.

'And more will be found in her.' I sighed. 'She's cheated the gallows, of course. And the public won't like that. But a jury would have found her insane.'

'Far better like this,' said Mansel. 'I mean, if she hadn't taken her life, the subsequent proceedings won't bear thinking about. I felt quite sick when he mentioned the women police. By the way, you'll have to tell Jenny.'

'Yes,' I said. 'It's my job.'

I told her upstairs in her bedroom, when she came in.

'Listen, my darling,' I said, 'Falcon has been and gone. I think he'll be back tomorrow.'

'Been and gone?'

'While you were out, my sweet. He couldn't wait.'

Jenny regarded me.

'What's happened, darling? You look so terribly grave.'

'It's all over, Jenny. The Mother Superior did it.'

'Richard!'

'She confessed and then took Mafra. There's not a shadow of doubt.'

Jenny burst into tears...

I let her weep in my arms.

When she was calm again–

'It was better that way, my darling.'

My wife did not seem to hear me. Her eyes were looking out of the window at something she only could see.

'Now it's all over,' she said, 'please let me go to the Home. I think, perhaps, they'll let me see Rosemary. I'm sure she loved Lord St Amant and he loved her. Before the war, I mean. And then, when she thought he was dead, she took the veil.'

As soon as I could speak–

'Did she hint at such a thing? When you met her at Buckram, I mean.'

'Oh, no. But I'm sure I'm right.'

Now that I had been told it, so was I.

At a quarter to four on Sunday, I brought the Rolls to the gates of the Nursing Home. These were shut.

A constable stepped to my side, and I showed him Falcon's card.

'That's quite all right, sir.'

He nodded to a gardener inside, who opened the gates.

As I brought the car to the doors–

'I may be some time, my darling.'

'Jenny,' I said, 'I don't come into this. You're to stay just as long as you please. I've brought a book to read and I don't care how long I wait.'

Jenny smiled and nodded.

'I thought you'd say that,' she said.

'Oh, and here's a note from Falcon. Don't tell me what he says.'

Jenny read it and nodded. Then she folded it again and gave it back to me.

As I saw her out of the car, Sister Geneviève appeared at the head of the three, low steps. At least, I was sure it was she: and when we were back at Maintenance, Jenny said I was right. I saw her greet my wife. Then they turned together and passed out of sight.

It was nearly six o'clock before Jenny reappeared at the head of the steps.

As I left the car—

'Come, Richard,' she said.

I mounted the steps and followed her into the hall.

There a sister was standing. Again I knew who it was.

'This is my husband – Sister Helena.'

I bowed, but she put out her hand, and I took it in mine.

When I met her eyes, I saw a quiet, grave smile on the peerless face. Falcon was right. She might have been the Madonna.

Suddenly I felt very humble and very much of the earth. At the risk of sounding foolish, I felt I should be on my knees.

A quotation came into my mind. 'These are they which came out of great tribulation … and God shall wipe away all tears from their eyes.'

For a moment we stood in silence. Then–
'God bless you both,' she said in her low, sweet voice.

And then she was gone…

Jenny never spoke, until we were halfway home, but when we had left the grounds, she slid her arm through mine and held it tight.

At last–

'She wanted to see you, darling. You see, she remembered me, and she wanted so much to be able to remember you. She said she would pray for us both as long as she lived.'

After dinner that Sunday evening, Falcon took up his tale.

'I always felt very strongly that the murder had been committed by somebody on the spot. That is why I never fancied the Duchess. But it was Sir William's letter that started me off. This, as no doubt you perceived, put quite a fresh complexion upon the case. It gave it, let us say, a new look. For it made it perfectly clear that whoever did the crime was either connected with medicine or had some connection with France. Paterson was much in my mind. But, if indeed it was he, then he was a past master of the art of roguery. I set him aside for the moment and looked elsewhere. Always excepting the Duchess – and I must confess that she seemed to be leading the field by a good many lengths – there was only Dallas left, so far as I knew. And he was bed-ridden. I decided that I must find out who else of those in the running had some connection with France.

'That was on Friday morning, not quite three full days from the time the murder was done.

'Now for Saturday morning. Until that Saturday morning, the idea, which proved the correct one, had never entered my head.

'You'll remember that the Mother Superior had asked me to come and see her at half past ten. I hoped and believed this meant that, after a talk with her, Sister Josephine was going to open her mouth. As you know, I kept the appointment and I told you all that was said. But I didn't comment upon it. Neither did you. There was one obvious comment: but when you didn't make it, I knew you were waiting on me. And I valued your reticence, for I wasn't ready to comment – even to you.'

(Falcon did us more than justice. Mansel and I had, both of us, noticed the point: but had dismissed it, as being of no account.)

'The obvious comment was this. *Why wasn't Sister Josephine there?*

'I mean, she should have been there, to tell me herself. I could have asked to see her, but that would have made it clear that I wasn't content. And that was the last impression I wanted to give.

'I hope you will try to imagine my state of mind. Without any warning at all, a flash-light had illumined for an instant a bleak and terrible prospect of which I had never dreamed. *Why wasn't Sister Josephine there?* The temptation to weigh the implications of her absence was insistent: but I knew that I must not do that. I must concentrate as never before upon the conversation about to take place. And so I did.

'I listened to every word that the Mother Superior used. I marked the inflections she gave them. I watched her face and her hands. And when it was over, I wasn't satisfied. Our relations had certainly improved: but now they seemed to me to be improving too fast. I had done my best: but now she was making the pace. "We were perfectly right, Superin-tendent." "Well, now, I must make a confes-sion." "So you see, the fault was mine." And then, at the end, she actually rallied me...

'Now, if Sister Josephine had been there, and the woman had spoken like that when the girl was gone, I should have thought nothing of it. I had been attentive on Friday – had spared her and Sister Helena all I could. And so she wished to convey the favourable impression she had formed of my solicitude. But Sister Josephine hadn't been there. And so I began to wonder whether the Mother Superior was playing a game – seeking to win my goodwill, for that, of course, is the finest defence in the world.

'As I left her room, a sudden, sharp suspicion leapt into my brain. For all I knew, she had never questioned the girl. I could hardly wait to see Sister Geneviève. And yet I knew I must wait. If she liked to come to me, well and good. If not, then I could approach her on my return.

'I walked out of the house, proposing to prove the meadows for a quarter of an hour. As I went, I surveyed the position. I wanted to be quite sure that my values were sound. You see, a sudden idea will sometimes blind the brain. It's so attractive – dazzling – you don't see some glaring flaw that will knock it right out. But so far as it went, I could find no fault in this. And so I applied my touchstone. Had the Mother Superior any connection with France?

At once a true flashlight flared. Of course you've already seen it. I tell you, I felt ashamed. I'd let the fact go by me without a thought. St Geneviève, of course. I think she's my guardian angel, in human shape. "He used to speak French with her. I don't know what he said, but one day she laughed outright."

'Now that was of great importance. It meant two things. First, that she could speak French extremely well. Many people can speak a language that is not their own.

But those who can jest in that language are very few. Secondly, it meant that St Amant knew that she was a mistress of French.

'I didn't tell you, but I went to see Dallas at once.

'"Good morning, Superintendent. You don't come to see me for nothing. What can I do?"

'I sat down and crossed my legs.

'"You can cast your memory back."

'"Oh, dear. I'll do my best."

'"Except for the sisters, you were the only person to talk with St Amant here."

'"Paterson."

'"True. I'm not counting him. St Amant talked to you as a fellow patient, you see."

'"So he did."

'"He spoke of France. You asked him to come and see you next time he passed that way."

'"Not France – Paris. I'm being precise."

'"Quite right. I want you to be. Had you any mutual friends? In Paris, I mean."

'"He mentioned the Vicomte de la Lattrie, with whom, he said, he had stayed. He has a big stable and an attractive wife. I mean, very gentle and charming. They are among – not my friends, but my acquaintances. He and I have nothing in common. I like the Vicomtesse very much. I said as much to St Amant, and he agreed with me. 'She's too good for him,' he said. Between you and me, that's putting it very low."

"'Anybody else?'"

'Dallas thought for a moment. Then he shook his head.

"'That's not to say that we hadn't. The probability is that we had. But nobody else was named. For instance, he almost certainly knew the Marquis and Marquise de Ste. Hermine. He is a power at Longchamp. And they are delightful people. The Marquise had an English mother. I can't venture to claim them as friends, but I have dined at their house and they've lunched with me."

"'Why did he mention de la Lattrie?'"

"'I told him where I lived. An apartment in the *Rue de Berri*. And he said at once, 'You're a neighbour of the de la Lattries.' I've stayed with them."

"'I quite understand. Well, thank you very much.'"

'He pointed to the paper beside him.

"'Dracona attends an inquest. Have they made a mistake? Or was it really she?'"

"'It was indeed.'"

"'Was she summoned?'"

"'No.'"

"'Did you suggest it?'"

"'Oh, no.'"

"'Well I'm – Almost you persuaded me to employ a *cliché*. Let us say that I am greatly surprised.'"

"'Why d'you say that, Mr Dallas?'"

206

'"Well, even I should prefer not to grace a Coroner's Court. As for Dracona... The steps to Dracona's throne are very steep. (You've taken them at a bound, but you are a superman.) They're very hard to climb, and I had supposed they were equally hard to descend. I shouldn't have said she very often tried. I mean, I had the impression that she was far too exalted – in her conceit – to be so much as aware of the sordid side of life. Yet of her own free will she submitted herself to the greedy stares of the vulgar, the gaping mouths of the morbid, the horrid circumstance which belongs to the Coroner's Court."

'I laughed and got to my feet.

'"I confess it surprised me," I said. "To tell you the truth, I think it did her infinite credit."

'Dallas raised his eyebrows.

'"Oh, yes. You must hand it to her – 'whose blood is very snowbroth'. It was a most handsome gesture."

'As I left his room, I wasn't so sure that it was. It might have been made to impress me – as it most certainly did.

'When I got to the Yard that Saturday afternoon, I called for reports from France on the ladies that Dallas had named. The French system is very useful. As, of course, you know, everyone has a *dossier* – everyone living in France. That *dossier* belongs to the police and is seen by no one else. If Dallas leaves Paris for Dinard, his *dossier* follows him there. And if, for instance, he was in the Baccarat Room, when a loser left the table to take his life, the fact would appear in his *dossier* – the fact that he was there when the fatal losses were incurred. And every movement is entered. I hadn't much hope that I should learn anything of value, but I had to find out how it was that St Amant knew that he could converse in French with the Mother Superior.

'That night, after dinner at home, I reviewed the startling impressions which I had that day received. They looked less startling then. Still, they were certainly striking. To be perfectly honest, they didn't amount to much. They had done no more than bring the woman into the running. If she was indeed the – culprit, I had still a long way to go. I began to look for a motive... But I didn't get very far, and I had a feeling that I should do better to wait.' Falcon paused there and looked round. 'In my particular job, I always think speculation a great mistake. It's very tempting sometimes; but it wastes a lot of time and it can be dangerous. After all, I had something to go on ... something which I had smelted in the traditional way ... not something thrust ready-made into my hands.

'I told you of my visit to Curfew and how on Monday morning I drove to the Yard.

They had nothing for me from France, but that was natural enough. Requests which are made on a Saturday afternoon seldom receive attention for thirty-six hours. Still, I wanted to see the papers and other things.

'Mafra had the Press beat. One paper alleged that it came from the Belgian Congo. Another that it was Burmese – and used on the tips of arrows in 1824. A third declared that Mithridates took it, when all other poisons had failed to take his life.

'I saw the AC of course. I had said nothing on Saturday, because, before I spoke, I had wanted time to think. But now it was right he should know the line I was on.

'When I told him, he covered his face.

'Then he said–

'"Go straight ahead. No fear or favour, Falcon. Straight ahead. If you prove to be right, the scandal will be too awful. That can't be helped. The country demands vengeance, and the country is right." He pointed to a pile of letters. "They come in by every post."

'He picked one out of the pile and gave it to me.

The Lord High Commissioner of Police,
Scotland Yard,
LONDON

MY LORD,
I'm only a poor old woman, but his dear

lordship used to buy his race-card from me. Course I no he had one, but hed always pretend he hadnt sos not to let me down. Why, Nellie, hed say, its good to see you agane. And ed always take is hat orf. Take is hat orf to me. And now some bloody murderers took is lovely life. Say youll get him, sir. Tell an old woman the crule beast ll be hung. It's all I want to live for. To no hes dead.

Yours respectful
OLD NELLIE.

'I handed the letter back and looked him full in the eyes.

'"If I am right, and a scandal could be avoided..."

'"Falcon," he said, "you've got to be very careful. I know what you mean, of course. But listen to me. If they think you let her do it, they'll want your blood."

'"I should never do that, sir," I said. "I was too well groomed."

'"I leave it to you," he said. "You've never failed us yet."

'I thought that was very handsome.

'Then he said that a VIP desired to see me in person at five o'clock.

'"Oh, dear," I said.

'"I know it's the devil," he said. "But we can't refuse."

'"I hope you'll be present, sir."

'"We shall go together," he said. "But remember he isn't a policeman. Don't open your mouth."

"'I quite understand."

'After that we arranged a code to be used on the telephone. Amongst other things, if I said that I wanted two copies of a map of Wiltshire, it really meant that I wanted two women police.

'I left him then and rang up Harford Almack. He did the operation on Lord St Amant's jaw. He was out of Town, but his secretary fixed an appointment for nine o'clock the next day.

'Well, you know I saw Berryman. Soon after he'd crawled out, the reports from Paris came in.

'As I had feared, these told me nothing of value. Both ladies were well-known figures and entertained a good deal. Both were resident in Paris and both had homes in the country to which they sometimes repaired. Madame de la Lattrie had spent the war at their place not far from Nimes. Madame de Ste. Hermine had taken her children to the States and had only returned in 1945.

'That evening I went to Whitehall. The Press had got it, of course – there's security for you. I counted seven cameras, when I got out of the car. The AC was furious. Just before we took our leave, he fairly let out.

"'I think you should know, sir," he said, "that no one in Scotland Yard had the faintest idea that we were coming here. And we went round by Drury Lane, instead of driving direct. Yet the pavement was crammed with reporters when we arrived."

'"Good God," says the VIP.

'"It means there's a leakage somewhere. Somebody in this office has been or will be paid for informing the Press that Superintendent Falcon would be here at five o'clock. Forgive me for telling you, sir, but I'm only doing my job."

'A lord-in-waiting was present, so I rather fancy there'll be the devil to pay. But the VIP behaved like a gentleman.

'"Of course it was your duty," he said. "And it is my duty now to apologize. And I'll tell you this, Sir George – somebody's going to be fired, and I don't care who it is."

'The interview itself was nothing. He hardly asked a question. He simply told me that I was to go all lengths. "If you want to question some man, and he's in Indo-China, we'll get him back. But I am counting on you to deliver the goods. From what I know of you, I believe you will."

'The AC asked me to dine with him at his Club, but I said that, if he would excuse me, I'd rather spend the evening alone. So I went back and bathed and changed and had dinner served in my flat. Then I told my fellow, Mole – I'm doing my best to make him like Carson and Bell – to take any calls that came and to say I was out, except to Sir

George, Rogers and you. Even the Yard could wait till I chose to go to bed.

'Then I put up my feet, took out the envelope which I had found in the wall-safe, laid it beside me on the sofa and began to think.

'From the moment that Berryman had so offensively – in my eyes – declared who Sister Helena was, it had always been in my mind that, if he had recognized her, St Amant certainly had. And I had always felt that, behind this recognition there might be lying something which I should be glad to know. But, except in the last resort, I felt that I must not explore such highly sensitive ground. I didn't even dare to set inquiries afoot, as, of course, I could have done: for romance has a strong appeal and an even stronger scent. However careful you are, it always seems to find its way into the Press.

'I'd looked them both up in *Burke*. St Amant was slightly more than three years older than Lady Rosemary Vernon. In 1939 he was twenty and she was seventeen.

'I'd already examined his wrist-watch. Inside the cover of this was engraved the one word *Jo*. This had been copied from writing, as such inscriptions very often are.

'Then I slit the envelope open.

'I did so heavily. The pitiful dead are so helpless. And I was flouting the very earnest desire of a man that was dead. I hoped that he would forgive me.

'It contained two documents, both of which confirmed what I'd come to suspect. Both were love-letters and both were from Rosemary Vernon, written at different times. The first was written in the summer of 1939. It showed that they were secretly engaged, and that they were to declare their engagement as soon as she was eighteen. That'd have been in September 1940. The second was written in 1942. It was the most anguished document that I have ever read. She'd got it smuggled out of some convent. "It's wicked of me to write, but I've got to let you know... When they said you were dead, life stopped... I thought, by doing this, I'd be nearer you..."'

There was a long silence.

I stole a glance at Jenny. She was sitting still as death. But her lovely head was high and, though she looked very grave, she showed no sign of grief. That she had known what was coming was clear to me.

Falcon continued slowly.

'The handwriting was that of the wrist-watch.

'It seemed that I had uncovered another facet of this dark and terrible jewel.

'Two nights before, I had refused to let myself look for a motive. It would have been speculation. But now it was not. I do not believe that two beings so deeply in love, whom Fate had so brutally sundered and then so brutally thrown together again, could have helped responding to each other's bitter cry. I mean, it's unthinkable. Very well. If this was so much as suspected by the Mother Superior, I was sure that, to crush the relation, she would have gone all lengths.

'I am quite prepared to admit that that might not have done for a jury; but it was ample for me. I knew the woman's outlook. To her, the way of Nature was the way of sin. A bleak, forbidding, heartless interpretation of life. The flesh was made to be mortified. Love was nothing but lust – an emotion, the bare thought of which was a mortal sin. And once the vows had been taken, a soul was saved. Her flock were the children of Heaven. "But whoso shall offend one of these little ones..."

'Somehow she had discovered that that was what St Amant had done – a monstrous perversion of the gentle teaching of Christ. And so she had dared to assume the office of executioner.

'I had to pull myself up. As is so often the way, I was going too fast.

'I now had a first-class motive: but I still had a long way to go. First, I had to be sure that, beneath the frightful strain of such a tragic reunion, St Amant had broken down. Secondly, that the woman had reason to believe this was so. Thirdly, of her possession of Mafra.

'I'll deal with that at once.

'To prove possession might well be beyond my power. But I must be able to show that she might very well have possessed that terrible drug. And that was going to be one hell of a fence to leap. My only hope was some close connection with France. A French physician, perhaps. But that was no good. No physician would ever admit that he had supplied Mafra to anyone.

'I gave up thinking about it, and went to bed. Fate seemed to have taken charge and was guiding my steps. And so I would leave it to her.

'On Tuesday morning I drove to Wimpole Street.

'I took to Almack at once – a nice, sympathetic man. He was greatly upset, as was natural enough. He'd fallen for St Amant at once. The perfect patient, he called him.

'"Tell me," I said, "who chose that nursing home?"

'"I did," he said, "for my sins. For two or three years I've sent my patients there. Of course it's very expensive: and then again they won't take everyone. But it seemed the very place for a man like that. When I mentioned its name – we call it Ne'er-do-well – he said, *Oh, I've heard of that. Somebody told me her aunt was the Mother Superior. Now who on earth can it have been? I have an idea she was French.* I said at once that the

Mother Superior was English, as were they all. *That's funny,* he said. *I'm sure she was French, because I remember her laughing about the name. She said it was impossible to pronounce, impossible to spell, and that, if you contrived to do either, you found you were being rude.* Rather good that, you know."

'"He didn't say who it was?"

'"No. He couldn't remember."

'"Never mind. Of course you know Paterson."

'"Oh, very well. I should think he's been very helpful. A first-rate man."

'"He has been very helpful," I said.

'"It's an excellent job, and of course he's very well found and very well paid; but not everyone would stick it. I mean he has to conform. The Mother Superior rules with a rod of iron."

'"I'd gathered that."

'After a little more talk, I thanked him and said goodbye.

'I confess that I was excited – a thing which no detective should ever be. I had really got something now. You'll remember Dallas' words – "The Marquise had an English mother." I had no doubt that it was the Marquise de Ste. Hermine who was the woman's niece.

'When I got back to the Yard, I examined again the report which the French had sent. "French by birth... Born in Paris in 1902...

Married in 1921... Three children... Remarks – of good report."

'Then I drafted a further request. I asked for details of her movements since 1935. Also for full particulars of her mother: maiden and married names, movements since 1935 etc. I marked this VERY URGENT.

'Then came one of those trying periods of waiting. I saw the AC of course, and I put through a call to Rogers – really for something to do. All quiet at Ne'er-do-well. I didn't dare leave the Yard, in case the report came in.

'It arrived at four o'clock – and a great disappointment it was.

'First, except for her visit to the USA, 1939–1945, Madame Ste. Hermine had not been out of France since 1935.

'Secondly, her mother, the Comtesse de Jeige, had died in 1949 and her *dossier* had been destroyed.

'In some impatience, I sent another request: this for Madame de Jeige's maiden name. At least, they must be able to furnish that. Meanwhile, I had to get on. If France couldn't help me, I'd got to help myself. I enlisted the help of 'Records'.

'I spoke to the AC first and told him that the search to be made might keep them up half the night.

'"That doesn't matter, Falcon. I'll speak to Burwash, myself."

'Burwash was ready for me. But when I gave him the slip, he bit his lip.

The Countess de Jeige. British Subject by birth. French by marriage. Presumably resident in France. Maiden name, not known. Died 1949. INFORMATION REQUIRED: What visits, if any, were paid by the above to the British Isles between 1935 and 1949. Details.

'"We must work back," Burwash said. "I'm afraid it may take some time. If she came in between 1938 and 1946, Ewing will have her down."

'"That means that, between those dates, she was vouched for?"

'"Yes – with or without her knowledge."

'"That's what I want."

'"We'll get on to it at once."'

Falcon looked round.

'This urgency may surprise you. You may be wondering why it was so very important that I should receive this information as soon as ever I could. The answer is this. I dared not postpone my return to Ne'er-do-well. On Thursday morning at latest, I must be back. For I had people to see – and irons grow cold. Now when I went back, things might move very fast – as, in fact, they did. But unless I knew that the woman *could* have had Mafra, I should not dare act. And if I was held up like that – well, I don't say that things get out, but danger has a scent of its own. Quite a lot of people can smell it. I'm sure that both of you will bear out what I say.'

'I will, indeed,' said Mansel. 'I think it's instinct, Falcon. More than once that instinct has saved my life.'

Falcon nodded.

'In a guilty person, that instinct can be very strong. Because their senses are tuned to the particular wavelength on which the whisper of danger can be heard.

'Well, I went back to my room. There I sat down, read through all my reports and made a very full note. In this I set down every tiny detail that could be construed as bearing out my belief that the Mother Superior had taken St Amant's life. Of course, there were serious gaps. Whether those would be closed, I could not tell.

'At half past seven I went back to talk to Burwash...

'Ewing and Burwash found it at a quarter past eight. Exactly what I wanted – much more than I had hoped.

28th June 1940. Entry at Liverpool. Victoria Mary. Countess de Jeige. French by marriage, British Subject by birth. References: – Sir Evelyn Scrope, Fennings, Broadway, Friend: The Mother Superior, The Nursing Home, Ne'er-do-well, Sister.

'I caught the AC as he was leaving his room.

'"Evelyn Scrope," he said. "Yes, he's all right. I think Lady Scrope is dead. He's getting on: he must be nearly eighty. A very nice, gentle, man. Are you going to ring him up?"

'"I want to," I said. "I want to ask him to see me tomorrow at ten o'clock."

'"I'll do it for you, Falcon."

'"It's very good of you, sir."

'Twenty minutes later my telephone rang.

'"AC speaking, Falcon. Scrope will be happy to see you, between eleven and twelve."

'"I shall be at his gates, sir, sharp at eleven o'clock."

'"I thought you would. Some things won't wait. And then you'll go on to Wiltshire. Well, here's the best of luck."

'"Thank you, sir."

'"Goodbye."

'I enjoyed the ride down to Broadway. In a police car, it doesn't take so long.

'Sir Evelyn was perfectly charming.

'"You may command me, Superintendent. Ask whatever you please. I knew Lord St Amant's father very well."

'"Thank you," I said. "And now I'll go straight to the point. I want some information about the Comtesse de Jeige."

'He raised his eyebrows and smiled.

'"About Vicky?" he said. "You couldn't help liking Vicky. You know she's dead?"

'"In 1949."

221

""'48 or '49. You're probably right. She was a very old friend – at school with my wife. I must have met her first in the early nineteen-twenties."

"'I assume that she lived in Paris."

"'That's quite right. I think it was in Paris that I met her first. But she was often in England. You know, of course, that she was an English girl."

"'Yes."

'He smiled.

"'The strange thing is that no one would ever have dreamed that she wasn't clean-bred French. I heard a Lord Chancellor once congratulate her on her beautiful English. She gave him a bewitching look. Then she broke into Cockney. You ought to have seen his face."

'We laughed together.

"'It's clear," said I, "that she was full of fun."

"'She was, indeed. And very, very pretty. Altogether most attractive and excellent company. But she was very French."

"'What exactly d'you mean by that?"

"'Oh, nothing to her discredit. But she had that careless elegance of manner which only the well-bred Frenchwoman seems to possess. Then, again, she was a realist."

"'You knew her well, Sir Evelyn."

"'Oh, yes, very well. She stayed with us more than once. I never cared for her husband. I thought him rather spineless. But I was wrong."

'"Why d'you say that?"

'"When France surrendered, he forced her out of the country against her will. He drove her to port after port, to get her on board some ship – without success. At last he got to, I think, St Jean-de-Luz. And there he found a ship: and on that, being British by birth, she was taken aboard. Then he turned round, dismissed his chauffeur and drove back the way he had come. He was never heard of again. I think he knew how to die."

'"Did you see her when she arrived?"

'"She came straight to us – and stayed for three or four months. She arrived in some General's car. That was Vicky. Landed at Liverpool. Nothing but what she stood up in, and not one penny in her purse. But a General's car. How she did it, I've no idea. She was well over fifty then, but she had this amazing charm."

'"How did she react to the fall of France?"

'"She was greatly upset, of course. She'd never expected France to go as she did. But she'd always been sure they'd be beaten. And she was entirely convinced that England would be overwhelmed. She knew we should never surrender, but she was perfectly certain that Hitler would have his way. *She had poison all ready to take, when the Germans arrived. She pressed some upon my wife:* but she only laughed and told her to wait and see.""

There was a little silence.

Then Falcon went on.

'"You say that she stayed with you for three or four months."

'"Yes. Then she took a flat in London – Hampstead, I think. You see, her father was rich, and all her private fortune was in the hands of Trustees – in England, of course."

'"I see. Did you see her again?"

'"Oh, yes. Several times. She used to come down for a week. But she had a lot of friends."

'"Did she go to see her sister?"

'"At Ne'er-do-well? Not very often, I think. They had very little in common. I know she went once. That was soon after she got here."

'"While she was staying with you."

'"Yes. Some time in July, 1940. Petrol was difficult, but we managed to get her there. I think she felt it was her duty. You see, she was then convinced that the German onslaught was only a matter of days, and she felt that, once it had come, she would never see her sister again."

'"I don't suppose you went with her."

'"As a matter of fact, I did. I didn't go in, of course. I sat in the car outside."

'"She wasn't long."

'"Not very long. Three quarters of an hour, perhaps. I think, you know, she was glad to get it over. I remember that when we were leaving, she heaved a sigh of relief. *En voilà pour un an!* she said. *If we are still alive. At least, I have done my duty.* That was her way, you know. She would leap between English and French in a most attractive way."

'"No love lost there."

'"I don't think there was. Her sister was older than her by five or six years. I remember her saying once, 'Blood may be thicker than water, *mais elle n'a pas de sang dans les veines. She has one use for my visits – and only one. She loves to air her French.'*

'"Did you ever meet her sister?"

'Sir Evelyn shook his head.

'"No." He got to his feet, moved to one of the windows and stood looking out. "My dear wife died in that home. A major operation. I don't think she could have survived. She was there because she and Vicky had been such very close friends. And she had known the sister, when she was young. The sister, the Mother Superior, never came near her once. If she had been herself, she would have laughed it off. But, being so ill, she felt it. It was unkind, you know."

'"It was brutal," I said.

'"That's how I saw it. Ah, well. It's all over now."

'"She knew who she was."

'"Oh yes. I'd written to her. We didn't expect special treatment, but it was such a smack in the face. Only a harsh and unconscionable woman could have done such an unkind thing."

'After a moment or two, he turned and came back to his seat.

'"Tell me this, Sir Evelyn. Why was Madame de Jeige so sure that the Germans would win?'

'He shrugged his shoulders.

'"She'd adopted the French outlook. She felt that nothing could stand against the mighty machine which Hitler had made. She'd a good deal to go on, you know. If they could have crossed The Channel, it wouldn't have been too good.'

'"And she had poison all ready?"

'"Yes, indeed. She didn't trust the Boche."

'"But where had she got it from?"

'"Some doctor in Paris, I believe. He supplied it for that very purpose. I imagine he picked his patients – I hope he did. She assured my wife it was painless and very swift."

'"She didn't say what it was called."

'"I don't think so. My wife was rather shocked at her having such stuff. And she begged her to keep it locked up. I remember her telling me that."

'I left the matter there – as well I might. To my great relief, he gave no sign of connecting the questions I'd asked with St Amant's death. But he's getting on, of course: and he is so quiet and gentle that I can well believe that murder is one of those things upon which he dislikes to dwell. So I guided him on to his friendship with Lord St Amant's father.

""I knew him well," he said. "We used to fish together. His wife was a very sweet woman. I had a lodge in Scotland, and they used to come to stay. Neither got over the shock of Joris' death. The tragedy being, of course, that he wasn't dead. He got back in time to see them, but the damage was done. Lady St Amant was failing, and he was aged. But for that, I think he'd have been alive now. Still, he's been spared this tragedy." He sighed. "It's beyond me, Superintendent. To my mind, only a maniac could have desired to put such a man to death. But I mustn't interfere. It's nothing to do with me. And I'm perfectly sure that you'll see that justice is done. Sir George spoke so nicely of you. He said I should enjoy our meeting – and he was perfectly right. I do hope you'll stay to luncheon."

""That's very kind of you sir; but I've got to get on."

""Very well. I'm not going to press you. You know your business best. A glass of sherry and a biscuit, before you go."

""Thank you. I should like that."

""I didn't really want it: but I felt that I couldn't refuse...

'As we shook hands–

""I know you'll forgive me, Sir Evelyn, for

227

saying this. What has passed between us is secret. I'm sure I can count upon you."

'"Indeed, you can. Not a word of what has been said will pass my lips."

'I should have liked to lunch at *The Lygon Arms*. But I couldn't do that: so I stopped at a wayside inn about ten miles off. After a little persuasion, they gave me something to eat.

'And then I drove on here.

'As I went, I surveyed the position.

'The most formidable jump had been cleared. Fortune, for some strange reason, had played clean into my hands. She had given me full measure – far more than I had dreamed that I should ever receive.'

'You went out and got it, Falcon.'

'I followed a line, Colonel Mansel. The moment I learned that Madame Ste. Hermine was the Mother Superior's niece, I was sure that it was her mother that passed the stuff. And when I found that she'd entered just after the fall of France...

'I felt very badly about keeping you in the dark. But I wasn't ready to disclose the terribly sinister path down which I was being led. I felt I must tread it alone. I didn't even tell Rogers. To tell you the truth, I was most deeply shocked. And I think perhaps you'll agree that I had no right to talk, until I could prove what I said.'

'When you say you felt badly,' I said, 'I feel

ashamed. If ever it helped you to talk, well and very good. But we respected your silence. It's very handsome of you to tell us now.'

'So long as you understand...

'Well, I wasn't home yet. A very great deal was depending on Sister Geneviève. What had Sister Josephine told her? And then – worst of all – I must see Sister Helena. I truly dreaded that: but it had to be done. On what I learned from those two, was depending the completion of my case. And I wanted to see the reports which Paterson made: for they had a certain importance. All the same, things seemed to be working out.

'Well, I got back here, as you know on Wednesday afternoon. And that evening I told you of Curfew and Berryman.

'The next day I went to the Home at eleven o'clock. (From this time on, I shall cut out the routine stuff.) Before I did anything else, I went to see the Mother Superior.

'The woman was very cordial. I hope I may be forgiven for playing up.

'"I'm glad to see you back, Superintendent."

'"Thank you, madam. I hope you haven't been bothered, while I was away."

'"In no way. I trust your visit to London was not paid in vain."

'"Not altogether, madam. But a case like this takes time. So many exhaustive inquiries have to be made. And I have a request to make."

"'Pray make it, Superintendent."

"'You have, of course, a record of the patients who enter this home. I should very much like to see it."

"'Of course. Ask Dr Paterson. The porteress has one, too. But his is the record to which I always refer.'"

Falcon stopped there and looked round.

'Pure camouflage, of course. But it was of the greatest importance that she should get no ideas.

'We talked for a few minutes more, and I took my leave.

'Then I found Paterson.

"'What would be a good time," I said, "for me to visit your house?"

"'Between four and five, Superintendent. I'm seldom wanted then. Will you come this afternoon."

"'Yes, if you please. I'll be with you soon after four."

"'Very well. I'll give you tea."

"'That's very kind of you."

'Then I went in search of Sister Geneviève.

'I encountered her in the corridor. As soon as she saw me, she gave me her charming smile.

"'I'd very much like to have a few words with you. What time would you suggest?"

"'I'm off between two and four. What about

half past three – in B consulting-room?"

"'I shall be there,' I said.

'And so I was.

"'Well, Sister Geneviève, did you see Sister Josephine?"

'She nodded.

"'Poor girl,' she said, "she didn't know what to do. She said you'd spoken so nicely and begged her so earnestly not to keep anything back. And yet she did. I'm afraid it's of no importance, because, you see, it happened on Monday night. But you had begged her not to keep *anything* back. But she didn't like to tell you, with the Mother Superior there. You asked about the visits she'd had. And she told you as best she could. But she didn't mention the Mother Superior's visit. She felt it was for the Mother Superior to tell you that."

'I smiled.

"'I think that was very natural."

"'I was sure you'd understand. The Mother Superior came in on Monday night."

"'I don't think I asked about Monday."

"'No, but you said 'everything'. And that was enough for Sister Josephine. Just about half past eleven, on Monday night, the window curtains parted and the Mother Superior came in. She didn't speak. She looked at the patient and then at the patient's chart. Then she knelt and prayed for a moment, and then she rose and went out."

"'One of her routine visits.'"

"'Yes. I don't do night duty now, but it used to be one of her ways of keeping us up to the mark.'"

"'You never knew when to expect her.'"

"'That's right. But, as I say, it was Monday – not Tuesday night.'"

"'Exactly. Had it been Tuesday, the Mother Superior would naturally have told me herself.'"

"'Of course.'"

"'And that is all she was withholding?'"

"'I'm afraid so, Superintendent. She's painfully conscientious: but reason is not her strong point.'"

"'Never mind,' I said. 'I'm glad to have cleared it up. For I knew she was holding back something. And now I've another – another favour to ask. It's very, very important that I should see Sister Helena quite alone.'"

Sister Geneviève bit her lip.

"'You mean there was trouble last time?'"

"'Yes. The Mother Superior was very much displeased.'"

"'Need she know, St Geneviève? You see, the thing is this. The first time I saw Sister Helena, I saw her alone. And after a little, she talked quite naturally. The second time I saw her was in the presence of the Mother Superior. And both of us were constrained. Nice as she is to me, the Mother Superior's personality takes precedence of that of

232

anyone else. When she is present, I can't get on terms with the witness. And the witness, of course, is more embarrassed than I."

'"Yes, I see that. But, if it got round to her... I mean, it did last time."

'"Can't I see her by night?"

'"She's on duty then. From eight to eight you know."

'"A quarter of an hour ... on the terrace..."

'Sister Geneviève appeared to reflect.

'"It might be arranged. It would have to be late, Superintendent."

'"At any time during the night."

'"This very night?'

'"If you please."

'She glanced at her watch.

'"Will you come to see me again about half past five?"

'"Without fail."

'I left her then and went for a stroll in the meadows. I had ten minutes to spare before I saw Paterson.'

Falcon sat back and looked round.

'"Out of the mouth of babes and sucklings," he said. Poor, foolish Sister Josephine had furnished the very best evidence I had.

'First, the Mother Superior had told me a downright lie.

'Secondly, what was she doing on the terrace on Monday night? And why did she enter Number Three?

'Thirdly – and this is rather intricate –

233

when did Sister Josephine first give me cause to think that she was concealing something which I should know?'

'It was quite early on,' said Mansel. 'Before you dealt with the visits.'

'You're right, Colonel Mansel. It was. Let me give you the questions and answers – I looked them up.

'Tuesday night, between half past ten and two. Can you remember hearing any unusual sound – a sound, for instance, which you had not heard the night before?

'Oh, no, indeed.'

'Quite sure?'

'Yes, I'm quite sure.'

Falcon leaned forward.

'So she was. She had heard no sound, *which she had not heard the night before*. But she did hear that. The same sound as she had heard on Monday.

'And now for the other two questions.

'I'm almost sure that a sound was made or that a light was shown on the terrace on Tuesday night.'

She shook her head.

'Does that mean you can't help me?'

'Yes.'

'Those were the answers I suspected.

'And now for the truth, of which Sister Josephine had told exactly one half.

'On Monday night, greatly to her surprise, the Mother Superior entered from the ter-

234

race about half past eleven o'clock. Bolton saw the curtains parted. If you remember, he saw "a flicker of light". On Tuesday night, the girl was on the alert. Sure enough, she heard the step she had heard on Monday night. And she knew whose it was, although she didn't come in. And that was at a quarter to two … when Dallas saw the flash of a torch.'

'That's very fine, Falcon. A beautiful piece of deduction. And because of what happened that very Tuesday night, she was afraid to tell even Sister Geneviève.'

'That's my belief.

'Well, I went to see Paterson. I asked to see the record – just for the look of the thing. When I had studied that, I asked to see the reports.' Falcon took out two sheets. 'These are the two that matter – copies, of course.

Saturday
Terrace, Number Four
Lord St Amant.

Physical condition	*Excellent*
Mental condition	*Excellent*

Penicillin
A first-rate patient. Curiously reluctant to take any drug, either to induce sleep or to relieve pain.

Sunday
Terrace, Number Four
Lord St Amant.

> *Physical condition*   *Excellent*
> *Mental condition*   *Excellent*

> *Should be fit to leave on Friday. Has given me his word to take japonica, if in pain.*
> *Wakes in pain every morning at four a.m. (Curiously enough, so does Mr Dallas, the patient in Number Five.) Insists that some atmospheric change takes place precisely at that hour. I had not noticed this and think it unlikely.'*

Falcon laid down the sheets.

'Those reports were made out in the evening and rendered to the Mother Superior at eight a.m. the next day. She, therefore, knew that St Amant would take two japonica tablets at four a.m.

'Paterson gave me tea and showed me the house.

'Then I walked back to the Home, to see Sister Geneviève.

'As I entered the corridor, she came out of a room.

'"At midnight," she said. "Come by the meadows, please. She will be waiting at the foot of the terrace steps."

'"God bless you," I said.

'As you know, I kept the appointment.

'I'd brought a rug from the car: so we sat on the steps.

'Then I spoke very low.

'"Supposing your bell should go."

"'Sister Geneviève is on the terrace, in case the light comes on. If it does, she'll flash my torch.'

"'Good. Sister Helena, before I ask any questions, I'll tell you what I know. And please put your trust in me. If I could have helped it, I'd never have broken this ground." I could see that she was trembling. "I know that in 1939 you and Lord St Amant were secretly engaged." I heard her catch her breath. "And I know that you took the veil because you thought he was dead." She was breathing hard and fast. But I thought it best to go on. "Policemen aren't supposed to have feelings: but when I found these things out, they tore my heart." She put out a hand, as a child in search of comfort: I took it in mine. "Tell me, did he know you were here?'

"'No.'

"'Did you know he was coming?'

"'No. When I entered his room the first evening, it was the most awful shock. But he ... was so wonderful. He – gave no sign of recognition; but talked quite naturally ... as if – as if he'd never met me before. And after a day or two, I thought that he didn't know me. I simply couldn't believe that he could be so easy and natural, if really he did. And I was so very thankful. It hurt ... of course: but it was so much better that way.'

"'Did anyone know your story?'

"'Nobody here – unless it was written

down in my secret report."

'"Who would see that?"

'"Only the Mother Superior. I was so terribly afraid that she might notice my manner and look it up. I mean, I did my best; but – it was so hard to pretend that I wasn't upset."

'"D'you think she did?"

'"I – don't know, Superintendent. She sent for me on the Sunday after he came. When I got the summons, I – well, I was terrified. But she didn't mention Jo. She said I was looking pale and asked if I was ailing. And I said no. You need a tonic, she said. Tell Dr Paterson so."

'"And that was all?"

'"Yes."

'"Whether she knew or not, you couldn't be sure."

'"Yes. I – I didn't know what to think."

'"Did Lord St Amant maintain the composure he showed?"

'Her hold on my hand tightened.

'Then–

'"Was that the torch?" she whispered.

'"No. I'm watching the terrace. I'll tell you if it's flashed."

'There was a little silence. Then–

'"I think he broke down," I said.

'"Yes," she said. "You're right. It was on the Monday, when I went to give him his tablets and say goodnight. When I'd put the tablets down, he put out his hand and took mine. And when I saw the look in his eyes, I knew that he'd known all along."

'"Did you stay with him for a little?"

'"Yes. I think my senses left me – only for a moment, you know. And then I was down on my knees, with my head on his bed."

'"Did he speak, Sister Helena?"

'She nodded.

'"We were both beside ourselves... After a little, he asked if I would tell him the date on which I'd – I'd..."

'"Taken your final vows."

'"Yes. I told him the date. Then he said very gently, *They pulled a fast one, Romy. My return was in every paper three days before.*'

'There was another silence, which I could not have broken to save my life. For one thing only, I couldn't trust my voice. Mercifully, she went on.

'"I know that I fainted then. When I came to, I was sitting in the chair, and he was kneeling beside me, bathing my temples and face... Then he begged me to ... break my vows. He said that I had the right, because I'd been tricked. He said that he'd come and fetch me... We were to go to Italy, under another name ... and live in some tiny village, all by ourselves... And I said that I'd think it over ... and tell him on Thursday night... I was mad, of course. But..."

'"There's a limit to endurance," I said. "Not to physical endurance, because Death

239

intervenes. But mental agony knows no such relief. And so one has to go on – to the breaking point."

'I saw her nod.

'Then she continued slowly.

'"Suddenly I thought of my bell. But, mercifully, nobody'd rung. Still, I went away then and left him... When I came in the next morning, he was himself again."

'"And that was on Monday night."

'"Yes."

'"At eleven, or thereabouts."

'"Yes. I think I must have been with him for half an hour."

'I held her hand very tight. Then I let it go.

'"That's the last of my questions," I said. "But I'd like to ask you a favour, as we are here alone. I'm in desperate need of guidance. Please will you pray for me?"

'"Oh," she said. "Of what use are my prayers now?"

'"Perhaps I see more clearly than you. They're far more valuable."

'Her head went down... So she sat for a moment. Then she stood up, and I rose.

'"For what it is worth, I will – with all my heart."

'She turned and passed up the steps...

'After a moment or two, I made my way through the meadows and over the wall.'

There was a long silence.

At last–

'Well,' said Falcon, 'my case was now complete.

'For some reason or other, the Mother Superior's suspicions were aroused. So she sent for Sister Helena on Sunday. Not satisfied with her demeanour, she went herself to the terrace on Monday night. She was listening outside Number Four, when St Amant broke down. When the scene came to an end, lest she should be discovered, she entered Number Three. And when the coast was clear, she returned to her apartments – by the meadows, as she had come. She made up her mind that night to put St Amant to death.

'This was too easy. She still had the deadly poison, which her sister had passed to her just fourteen years before. Paterson's reports had told her that St Amant took his tablets at four a.m. And so, at a quarter to two on that dreadful Wednesday morning, she entered his room, took the japonica tablets and left two tablets of Mafra in their place.

'Motive, opportunity, means – all three were evident. Her step had been heard by Sister Josephine; and Dallas had waked to see the light of her torch. And I had found the tablet which she had dropped.

'The only question remaining was how to proceed.'

'The only question,' said Mansel.

'Exactly,' said Falcon. He sighed. 'I

thought I'd had problems before. But I'd never had one like this. And as if that wasn't enough, the Inquest would be resumed that afternoon. And I had to be there, for Sir William was coming down.'

'Oh, my God,' said Mansel.

'Yes. It was very trying…

'So much was at stake. First and foremost, justice had to be done. The woman must be arrested and charged with the crime. There, in a way, my responsibility came to an end. But that was all very well. As the AC had said, the scandal would be too awful. That couldn't be helped, and it didn't weigh with me. Mother Superior or mill-hand, she was a murderess. But two things did stand out – and the look of them made me blench.

'The first was this. If the woman came to be tried, Sister Helena must be called and she would have to reveal exactly what she had told me upon the terrace steps.

'The second was not so frightening, but it was almost as grave. If the woman pleaded not guilty, I had no doubt at all that she would get off.

'Let me set out my reasons for that belief.

'Sister Josephine would make a bad witness – and that is putting it low. What was much worse, hearsay is no evidence. And that would wash out almost all Sir Evelyn had said. He couldn't mention the poison. All he could say in court was that in July 1940 he had taken Madame de Jeige to visit her sister who was at Ne'er-do-well Home. If he could have told the Court what he had told me, his evidence, coupled with that of Sir William, would, I truly believe, have sent the woman down. But he couldn't do that. Repeat what his dead wife had told him? In the absence of the accused? The thing was absurd.

'And so I was faced with a question which, to be perfectly honest, was not for me to decide. The decision should have been taken by someone greater than I. And yet I dared not submit it. For one thing, I hadn't time. On Saturday morning at latest, I had to act. And, for another, no one was as qualified as I was, for I alone had been taken behind the scenes.

'The question was this. In view of the fact that the woman would be acquitted, if she was brought to trial, was it right to expose Sister Helena, who had already endured an agony not of this world, to an even more savage ordeal than those through which she had passed?

'Well, I didn't take long to decide.

'They could draw and quarter me; but, if I could prevent it, her piteous, heart-rending story should never come out.

'The thing was, how to prevent this; because, you see, I'd got to make the arrest. Of that, there was no question at all. I didn't mind being broken for using my discretion

243

and using it wrong: but this was as clear a duty as ever I saw. I couldn't do it on Friday, with the Inquest round my neck. But on Saturday morning at latest – I think I've said that already – the thing must be done.

'Well, now I was almost sure that, rather than stand her trial, the woman would take her life. And nothing could possibly be better. It was the ideal solution. *But she had got to take it before she was under arrest.* Apart from the fact that I'd given the AC my word, I could never allow her to do it. I simply had not the right. More, I should have to prevent her, if she tried.

'As you may well believe, Friday last was the most distracting day I have ever spent. Could I have had my way, I would have spent the day beneath one of the trees in your meadows, entirely alone. I needed peace and quiet, to hammer this problem out. I mean, it was critical. It demanded the deepest reflection. The course which I had to steer was more than delicate. The slightest mistake would be fatal, and I should be on the rocks. As it was, I had next to no time at all. The Inquest, which didn't matter, had to take pride of place. The Chief Constable, the Coroner, the local police – all had to be seen and talked to. And then Sir William arrived. And then the Inquest itself. And the Press – on the top of it all…'

'I couldn't have done it,' said I.

Falcon shrugged his shoulders.

'I don't know how I did it – and that's the truth. But I filched twenty minutes here and another ten minutes there. And, after what reflection I could muster, I decided to write the letter of which you know.

You will receive me tomorrow precisely at ten o'clock.

'In view of our pleasant relations, there could, I felt, be no mistaking at all what such wording meant. It was more than peremptory. It was the Law speaking. The mask was off.

'Now I thought it possible that her sister might have given her more than one dose of Mafra, so that not only she, but one of her flock could use it, if occasion arose. Of course, Madame de Jeige might not have had it to give. But she had pressed a dose upon Lady Scrope. And that had been declined. So it did look as though she had two, to give away; for her sister would have been in her mind from the very first. And if the Mother Superior had more than one, it would be easy for her to take her life. And if she meant to do this, she could do it before I came.

'But she didn't. She went one better.

'When I saw her sitting there, for a moment I thought I'd failed. And then I hoped and prayed that the poison was in her mouth. But when she went on talking, I gave up hope. I simply couldn't believe – and I had Sir

William behind me – that the poison, if it was there, would not have dissolved. I gave it every chance. And at last it was clear that I could wait no longer… And when she put up her hand and I caught her wrist, I really and truly believed that I had played and lost.

'And then … after all … I won.

'Or did she win? I don't know. Let's say that honours were even.

'The Inquest will be held on Tuesday. I shall be the principal witness. For the look of the thing, I've written her spoken confession down in my book. And I shall read it from that. I have, of course, omitted her reference to her statement. That will be suppressed.

'My letter will take some explaining. That can't be helped. I mean, it was pretty fierce. And why did I write it at all? I'd like to suppress it, too. But I can't do that. For if I do, why had she Mafra in her mouth?'

Mansel lifted his voice.

'I think you can weather that. You were dealing with an arrogant woman, who had to be shown the whip. That will account for the tone. Why did you write it at all? Because the arrest must be made in an active Nursing Home. Not in some house or office or busy street. In a Nursing Home, where people were dying or lying seriously ill. It was of the utmost importance that there should be no disturbance in such a place. Yet, knowing the woman, you thought it more than likely that she would resist arrest. So you wrote in the hope of confining her to her room.'

'That's very good, Colonel Mansel, I'm much obliged. As for the rest, I think it will work out all right. I shall begin with the traditional words, "Acting upon information which I had received." In view of her spoken confession, that covers everything. Sir William will disclose what he said in his private letter – that he had heard that Mafra could be held in the mouth. It's the Coroner's Court, remember; the rules of evidence there are not so strict. Besides, he can always say that he "had reason to think, though he couldn't be sure". And now that they know what to look for, I think the analysis will be completed by Monday night. So there will be no adjournment. Paterson will have to be called, but nobody else from the Home. But I shall be able to tell you more tomorrow. In any event, I believe we've cleared the last fence.'

Falcon paused there and knitted his brows. Then he went slowly on.

'I'm not going to read you her statement. In fact, I've left it in Town. It confirmed in every particular what I had discovered or believed. It added only one thing, of which I ought to have thought.

'Sister Helena's history appeared in her secret report. So did the name of the man with whom she had been in love – The Honourable Joris Eyot. That name went down on a list which the Mother Superior kept – "Patients not to be received".

'Not until St Amant had been in the Home for four days, did the woman take *Burke's Peerage* and look him up. Then, of course, she knew why Sister Helena was looking so wan.

'But the contribution it made was greater than that.'

Falcon paused again.

'It was the most brutal document which I have ever read. Pride, vainglory and hypocrisy stood out from every page. But charity – no. Not a vestige. Sister Helena, she called "the creature". "In response to my summons, the creature came to my room."

'I may be wrong, but when she found that St Amant was Joris Eyot, surely the least she could do – any human being could do, was to change Sister Helena's duty there and then. Put Sister Thérèse in her place – or somebody else. Instead, she spied upon her. Stood and listened on the terrace on Monday night. A very cruel woman. Deliberately cruel. And an *agent provocateur*.'

'Any sign of insanity, Falcon?'

'She was as sane as I am. "Suicide while temporarily insane"? Not if I can help it. The woman deserves to be branded with a verdict of *felo de se*. And murder. Wilful murder. But more of that tomorrow. Anyway, it's all over now, except for the mopping up.'

'Well, I hope you're proud of yourself. It's

quite the biggest thing that you've ever done.'

'Oh, I don't know. I had a lot of luck. The really anxious business came right at the end. And there my luck held.'

'Be fair to yourself,' said I. 'It wasn't luck that wrote the letter you sent. That was what did the trick. It was very, very clever. You knew exactly how she would react to that.'

'I thought I knew,' said Falcon. 'I couldn't be sure.'

'Let us say that your judgment was perfect.'

'So it was,' said Mansel. 'So was your handling of the arrest itself. Your timing was masterly. It's all very well to say that you had some luck. If you did – which I don't admit – then you induced that luck. What did Sir George say?'

'I'm glad to say,' said Falcon, 'that he was very pleased.'

On Monday evening, he took up his tale again.

'I've had a light day,' he said.

'I went to see Paterson first. He's shaken to his foundations. That she could have done such a thing had never entered his head – would never have entered his head in a thousand years.

'"She must," he said, "she must have been out of her mind."

'"She didn't give me that impression at any time. I saw you on Thursday last. If I had then suggested that she was – well, round the bend, what would have been your reply?"

'After a little–

'"If I'm to be honest," he said, "I should have thought *you* were mad."

'"Well, there you are," I said.

'"But why, Superintendent? Why did she kill Lord St Amant?"

'"Because she fell a victim to his irresistible charm. D'you know that he actually made her laugh aloud?"

'Paterson stared.

'"I've never heard her laugh; and I've been here for more than twelve years."

'"Sister Geneviève was there. And when the woman found that even she could not withstand his charm, she decided that such a man was a highly dangerous man ... who could do what he pleased with women ... and so, while she had the chance, must be put to death."

'"Wasn't that madness, Superintendent?"

'I shook my head.

'"Puritanism," I said. "She could have led the Ironsides of Cromwell's day."

'"Yes," he said. "You're right. She could have done that. I've had to protest to her about the hardships which she imposed on the Sisters from time to time."

'"That doesn't surprise me at all. Now listen to this."

'I read him her spoken confession.

'When I had done – "Yes," he said, "that's

her. Her conception of duty must always be right."

"'That's not madness," I said. "Vainglory, perhaps."

"'That's right," he said slowly. "Vainglory. She was vainglorious. Very much more than wise in her own conceit. Fancy her quoting Shakespeare right at the last."

"'Listen, Dr Paterson. I was sent here, to see, if I could, that justice was done. Under no pressure from me, the Mother Superior declared – almost boasted that she had done wilful murder, the murder of a brilliant, *innocent* man... She took *her* life, because she had no intention of standing her trial: in other words, she was determined to avoid the consequences of her crime. I don't think justice will be done, if so cold-blooded a woman is accorded the charitable verdict of 'temporary insanity.'

'Paterson appeared to reflect.

'Then–

"'You're right, Superintendent. Cold-blooded exactly describes her. She wasn't insane and she doesn't deserve such a verdict. If you ask for *felo de se*, I'll back you up."

'There was a little silence. Then–

"'Who's taken her place?" I said.

"'I asked Sister Geneviève to carry on. Someone else will be sent."

"'An excellent choice."

"'Yes, she's a very sweet woman and very

capable. A pleasure to work with, Super-intendent. No ill of the dead you know, but this wasn't a happy Home."

'"No human kindness," I said.

'"Not a vestige. Duty, duty, duty. And if ever duty was a pleasure, that was wrong."

'"A gaunt philosophy."

'I seemed to have cleared that fence, so I said goodbye and drove to Ne'er-do-well.'

'Forgive me, Superintendent,' said Jenny. 'I don't quite understand.'

'Why should you, Mrs Chandos? Let me explain. Paterson will be called at the In-quest. He was the doctor at the Home. If he was to hint that the Mother Superior's mind had given way, we shouldn't get a verdict of *felo de se*. And that, I was determined to have. The verdict of "Temporarily insane" is very often given, when it is quite untrue. That's done out of charity. But I saw no reason why it should be done in this case. The woman deserved no mercy, alive or dead.'

'Thank you. I do agree. I mean, she was really evil.'

'That's my belief.

'Then, as I say, I drove to Ne'er-do-well.

'For once in my life, I refused to talk to the Press. They'll have their show tomorrow.

'I saw the Chief Constable first. I told him she killed St Amant and had confessed her guilt. The poor man was quite overcome – and too much concerned with the scandal to ask any awkward questions. When I begged him to rely upon me, he nearly burst into tears. "I'm getting old, Superintendent. Such things are too much for me. I mean, she of all people... I'd as soon have suspected myself. Such a pillar of righteousness. The scandal will be too awful."

'Rogers dealt with the local police. I knew I could trust him there. "Don't worry the Superintendent. He'll lead the team tomorrow. But now he is very tired." "But did she do it, Chief Inspector?" "Yes, she did it all right. But not a word."

'Then I called on the Coroner.

'I told him the truth – shortly, advised him whom to summon and said he should have their statements by five o'clock.

'"Temporarily insane, of course."

'"That won't be my evidence," said I. "Or Dr Paterson's either. The woman was no more insane than you or I. It was wilful, cold-blooded murder. She found Lord St Amant attractive, and that was enough for her. If she could feel his charm, what about weaker vessels? The man was dangerous."

'Then I read him her confession.

'"Good God," he said. "D'you really mean *felo de se?*"

'"I certainly do," I said. "This is not a case for covering up. It was a monstrous crime."

'"Oh, I'm with you there, Superintendent. But – but *felo de se.*"

253

'"It's an honest verdict," I said, "which my evidence and that of Paterson will more than support – let us say, will commend. And the woman has cheated the gallows. Don't forget that."

'"Yes," he said. "Yes, that's right. She should have been hanged. But what a terrible business."

'After luncheon I drew up the statements. I had to risk that of Sir William: but I knew what I hoped he would say. Rogers and one policewoman will be called, but not Sister Geneviève.

'Then a call came through from the Yard, to say that Mafra'd been found.

'I drove again to the Home.

'Paterson read through his statement, suggested a few additions and finally said, "That's right."

'Then I called again on the Coroner, went through the statements with him and drove back here.'

'A light day,' said Jenny.

'Comparatively, Mrs Chandos. What we call routine work.'

'Well, I don't know,' said Jenny. 'I've seen Richard extended. I've known him go without sleep for more than forty-eight hours. But you never stop using your brain. Don't say you're going tomorrow. I hope you'll stay here a week.'

'I must go up on Wednesday. I should like

to come back on Thursday; and if I may spend the weekend here – that I should like very much.'

'If you'll do as I say.'

Falcon smiled.

'With that condition,' he said, 'I'm more than content.'

On Tuesday evening, Falcon had little to report.

All had gone very well. Sir William had been most convincing. Paterson had come to the scratch. A verdict of *felo de se*.

'The Press were so excited they actually left me alone. Sir William's evidence hit them between the eyes. "It seems that I was mistaken. My information was true. So long as its case is unbroken, Mafra can be held in the mouth. But the instant the capsule is swallowed, it will dissolve." And Paterson's, too. "I saw her, as usual, that morning at nine o'clock. Her behaviour was absolutely normal. She was cold and collected, as usual: asked questions and gave me instructions in the most ordinary way. I hadn't the faintest idea that there was anything wrong... In my opinion, she was as sane as I am: but she was always a law unto herself."

Mansel lifted his voice.

'If Sir William and Paterson hit them between the eyes, I rather fancy that you must have knocked them out. I mean, her confession alone...'

Falcon nodded.

'Yes, it was very strong stuff... The silence in Court was uncanny. I could see the pencils going, but nobody seemed to breathe... I must say I'm thankful it's over.

'Tomorrow morning I shall once again visit the Home. You see, I must take my leave. Then I shall drive to London. I hope to be back on Thursday in time for tea.'

So it fell out.

And on Thursday evening, Falcon concluded his tale.

'As I said I should do, I drove direct to the Home.

'First of all, I saw Sister Geneviève.

'As acting Mother Superior, she was using the room I had come to know so well.

'"I've so much to thank you for, St Geneviève. I'd like to leave it there."

'"That's right," she said. "I'd like to leave it there, too. But I shan't forget you, Superintendent. I don't know much of the world; but you have shown me an aspect of human nature of which, until I met you, I never dreamed."

'"St Geneviève," I said, "I've learned of you. 'For *duty* lives with kindness.'"

'She lowered her eyes. Then she rose to her feet and put out her hand.

'"Goodbye, Superintendent. Thank you for doing so handsomely all that you had to do." She hesitated. "Sister Helena would like to see you."

"'I'm at her disposal," I said. "But won't she be resting now?"

"'No. She's off all duty for two or three weeks. In a quarter of an hour she'll be in Consulting-Room C."

"'I shall be there." I hesitated. "St Geneviève, may I make her a little present? It's not really mine to give, but that's neither here nor there. It's nothing much – only an old wrist-watch."

'There was a long silence.

'Then–

"'Yes," she said quietly, "you may."

'I looked her full in the eyes.

"'What did I say just now?" As before, her head went down. "Goodbye, St Geneviève."

"'Goodbye."

'I went to see Paterson.

'After a little conversation, the doctor looked at me.

"'I've never asked how you discovered the truth. To be quite honest, I don't very much want to know. But I think you must have a fine brain."

'I shrugged my shoulders.

"'After all, it's my job," I said, "to find things out."

"'I know, I know," he said. "But – well, almost anyone else. I mean, she was above suspicion."

"'Murderers sometimes are.'"

"'I can't get over it,' he said.

'I smiled.

"'I've a lot to thank you for. You helped me no end.'"

"'Oh, I did very little.' He hesitated. "We were very lucky in you. We all feel that. I mean, it might have been awful. I quite expected it would be. But you – fitted in so well.'"

"'That's a very nice compliment.'"

"'It's perfectly true. And you – you made my path very smooth.'"

"'Is it a happier Home?'"

'Paterson's face lighted.

"'Indeed, it is. Of course, Sister Geneviève…'"

"'Is as sweet as she's good,' I said.

"'So she is.'"

"'One last request. D'you mind if I visit Dallas before I go?'"

"'Of course not, Superintendent. You don't have to ask my leave.'"

"'I'm an interloper now.'"

"'You'll never be that.'"

"'Goodbye.'"

'I went to Consulting-Room C.

'As I entered the room, Sister Helena rose to her feet. "I wanted to see you," she said, "before you went.'"

"'That was very sweet of you.'"

"'I don't quite know what to say – except

to thank you for being so kind to me."

'"You prayed for me, Sister Helena."

'"Yes, I did. I shall always pray for you."

'"You make me feel very humble."

'"Don't feel like that. It's – inappropriate."

'I took out an envelope containing St Amant's watch.

'"Sister Helena," I said, "I have Sister Geneviève's permission to give you this."

'She put out her hand, and I laid the packet in her palm. For a moment she looked at it. Then her left hand came up and closed over her right. So she stood, like a statue, not seeming to breathe…

'Then she lifted her head and put out her right hand.

'As I took it in mine, she was trying to speak.

'I smiled and spoke, instead.

'"I shall see Mrs Chandos tomorrow."

'Her beautiful eyes lighted.

'"Give her my love. And ask her to come again."

'"Consider it done."

'She held my hand very tight.

'"Goodbye and God bless you," she said.

'"Goodbye."

'I took my leave.

'When I entered Dallas' room–

'"What a man."

'"I'm here for nothing this morning."

'"I've deeply regretted that. I was in pain

259

that morning. But that's no excuse. I must be getting testy."

'"I should be more than testy, if I had to lie here, as you have, day after day."

'He offered me cigarettes. When I had lighted one, I took my seat.

'"Is this goodbye?" he said.

'"Yes. But I had to come and thank you. You contributed more than you know to the – the bringing home of the crime."

'"The flash on the terrace."

'"For one thing. I'm not going to say what it was, but you gave me some information of greater value than that."

'"God bless my soul."

'I smiled.

'"*The rest is silence,*" I said.

'"May I ask one question?"

'"Of course."

'"When first did it enter your head that it might be Dracona herself."

'"The same day that it entered yours. Last Saturday week."

'Dallas covered his face.

'"Is anything hidden from you?"

'"We arrived by different paths. But we got there about the same time. You're a man of the world, Mr Dallas, and so am I. Of not only the under-world."

'"She didn't allow for that. I mean, if I may say so, you're rather exceptional."

'"I've had advantages."

'"No other detective alive would have raised his eyes to her."

'"That was her strongest suit."

'Dallas pointed to *The Times*.

'"*Directly I saw you, I knew you were dangerous.*"

'"You're very shrewd, Mr Dallas. I hope your knee's getting well."

'"Thank you, it's slowly improving. I hope to be able to get on to the terrace next week. Just as well I was bed-ridden."

'I laughed and got to my feet.

'"That certainly ruled you out."

'I put out my hand and he took it and held it fast.

'"Goodbye, Superintendent. I wish I'd known you before. You know where I live in Paris."

'"If ever I'm there, I promise to look you up."

'"I suppose you know that you've done a most beautiful job."

'"Thank you," I said. "I'm glad it came out as it did."

'He let my hand go, and put his hand up to his eyes.

'"Came out as it did," he said. "Came out... What a man!"

'Both of us laughed then, and I made my escape.

'I bade the porteress goodbye and drove to Ne'er-do-well.

261

'There I arranged for the Inquest on Lord St Amant to be brought to an end tomorrow at two o'clock. That was simple enough. (I must attend, of course – I shall be the principal witness. But her confession, of course, will finish it off.) I wrote a note to the Coroner, gave it to the local Superintendent and left the rest to him. Then I collected Rogers and off we went.

'I saw the AC as soon as I got to the Yard.

'He seemed very satisfied.

'"It couldn't have been better!" he said. "A trial would have been too awful. As it is, she's branded and Justice has been done. A very good leader in *The–*. Makes that very point. Pays you a very nice tribute – as you most richly deserve. Will you dine with me tonight? The Director's going to be there. Just us three... Good. Let's say a quarter past eight. At four o'clock we've got to go to Whitehall.'

'"What, again?"

'The AC smiled.

'"The VIP wants to thank you. I've said he can tell the Press."

'"Oh, that's not fair, sir," I said.

'"I don't agree."

'The Press must have told the public. I really was quite ashamed. Uniformed police were there to control the crowd.

'The VIP spoke very nicely indeed.

'"A double triumph, Superintendent. Please believe that I'm very grateful indeed.

And full of admiration."

"'I was very fortunate, sir.'

"'From what I hear, you induced what luck you had. What should we do without you?"

'I didn't know where to look.

'I wanted to leave by the back, but the AC wouldn't have that.

"'They want to see you," he said.

'It was really very moving – not in my line. All trying to shake my hand or clap me upon the back. Reflected glory, of course. It shows how St Amant was loved.

'And so to dinner – at the AC's private house.

'The Director was very cordial, and after dinner of course I opened my mouth.

'At the last–

"'As it turned out," he said, "if she'd lived, we should have got home. Because you found more Mafra locked up in her chest of drawers. That would have sent her down. But you never expected to find it. You had no reason on earth to think it was there. Four doses of Mafra the Countess must have received. A positive armoury. Fancy any physician giving her that amount. She probably approached two physicians, and each of them gave her two. But what a nightmare business the trial would have been. That poor, unfortunate girl... It makes my blood run cold. Oh, no. Very, very much better to end as it did. Didn't the Coroner kick at a verdict of *felo de se?*"

"'I frightened him into it, sir. I said that Paterson and I were, both of us, going to swear that she was perfectly sane.'"

"'A masterly performance, Superintendent, from first to last. I was always sure that you would deliver the goods. But you did much better than that. You've really done everyone's job. I include the hangman. You've never brought me a carcase, as so many fellows do. That's not your way. And I've got to skin it and clean it and sometimes find it bad. Unfit for a jury's consumption. Your meat is always handed to me on a plate. So it would have been this time. That letter you sent her. Against all the conventions, of course. But master-strokes often are.'"

Falcon stopped there and looked round.

'I tell you these things, but not out of vanity. You know, even better than I, how very little the praise of the world is worth. But I wanted to complete the picture – for now I've done – of what I shall always consider much more than a case.

'And "picture" isn't quite right. I think it's more of a triptych, of which only you and I have studied the whole.

'Let's consider the outside first.

'The death of Lord St Amant was a catastrophe. In these most dangerous days, when men like Berryman are stoking the fires of class-hatred, which, as I happen to know, require no stoking at all, this nobleman's life issued a shining statement no communist dared deny. More. To the gentle youth of England, he set an inspiring example: he showed them how to behave. Such a man in these days was worth far more to his country than any politician or prelate, be they never so wise.

'Well, he was cut off in his prime. He was murdered, in a barbarous way. At once the eyes of England were focused on Scotland Yard. And if Scotland Yard had failed, she would not have been forgiven for years to come. Her very prestige was at stake.

'That's the outside of the triptych. What do we find within?

'In the first place, we find the truth. That lies in a love-affair, between a young god and goddess, each bearing a famous name – the saddest, most pitiful story that ever was told. We speak of "the irony of Fate". I will wager that not one in a million who uses that well-known *cliché*, has ever conceived an instance one half so savage as that which the centre panel so faithfully presents.

'Now for the lesser panels, one upon either side. The same figure appears on each. On the left, a Mother in God, whose cure of souls was rare, to whose charge Lord St Amant was committed – a truly notable figure, adorning her office, displaying an efficiency which had to be seen to be believed. On the right, a murderess, who took it upon herself to destroy the brilliant being whose charm had touched her heart. And when she had committed this fearful crime, lied, did her best to deceive me, sought, as she admitted, to print a false impression upon my mind ... to save herself from the consequences of her deed.

'I think you'll agree with me that this was more than a case. It was a terrible drama, a shocking tragedy. The evil which it has done is quite incalculable. St Amant's loss apart, a blow has been dealt to all convents, which men will talk of for years. "Them – nuns."

'That is why I have left nothing out. In such a picture as this, every tiny detail contributes to the amazing whole. It's like a painting by Memlinc, in which the expression of each of the many faces plays its part. Dallas, Bolton and Sister Geneviève: Selden, Sister Josephine, Paterson: the surgeon and Sir Evelyn, mildest of men.

'And no one but you and I has seen or will ever see the detail of all five panels of a triptych – a human document, such as I never expected to read myself.'

That was Falcon's summing-up, and I cannot better it. When he said it was not a case, that was perfectly true. I do not know what to call it. Perhaps, an event. And Falcon shaped its end.

On the following day, the Inquest on Lord St Amant came to an end. The proceedings were formal and took but a very short time. A verdict of wilful murder by Cecilia, Mother Superior, was returned. Out of consideration for her family, her true name was not disclosed.

By one consent, that evening we spoke no more of the Ne'er-do-well affair. But after dinner Falcon looked at us.

'You told me of Daniel Gedge. I should love to hear of some others with whom you dealt.'

Mansel laughed.

'You turn to small beer,' he said.

'I shouldn't call The Shepherd small beer.'

The Shepherd was Mansel's meat: and the rest of us sat and listened while he related quietly the brush he had had with him.

When he had done—

'The relief at the Yard,' said Falcon, 'when you reported his death, was very much more than marked. The gems that man got away with. And we never knew who he was. Formosa was suspected. But we had too little to go on, and the French refused to play. I think they fought shy of the man, as they did of Daniel Gedge. And he was a member of Walter's. I'm not in the least surprised. The AC always maintained that he was someone like that.'

Then we spoke of Friar.

'That was William's show,' said Mansel, and made me tell the tale.

When I had done–

'Friar was suspect,' said Falcon.

'That's a new one on me,' said Mansel. 'When I talked to James –, he said you had no idea.'

'He probably didn't know it: but Friar was down on my list. I've seen him myself in very queer company. But he never worked in England. Like The Shepherd, as you probably know, he belonged to a famous Club. But I knew that, to live as he did, he must have a handsome income which he didn't honestly earn. He'd pay big money at Christie's for *objets d'art*. A very hard case. We were very grateful indeed when you broke Biretta and Cain. They'd been a thorn in our flesh for several years. Cain was the driving force. He was rather like Baal, you know. But they were terribly slim. But we ought to have known Forecast. When you told us the truth of his hostel, we nearly died. The AC was simply furious. It was in –'s district. He was retired at once. And now, if you please, will you tell me of Number Four?'

'Ah,' said Mansel. 'Bullfinch. We used to call him Barabbas. He was an evil man.'

'He did murder by proxy,' said Falcon, 'again and again.'

'That was how Lord St Omer died. And

that set us off.'

Between us, we told how at last we were led to Barabbas and put an end to the man.

'There you are,' said Falcon. 'That was a thing which we could never have done.'

'You said,' said Jenny, 'that you would do as I said. I think you should go to bed. And tomorrow we'll all go fishing. On Sunday the Avons have asked us to bring you to lunch.'

I think Falcon truly enjoyed the next three days. He shared our very quiet life. The Avons made much of him: he was Jenny's obedient servant, as Carson and Bell were his. On Monday, at his request, we visited Adamant. The latter was out of humour: but Jenny talked to him and after a little, his head came out of his box. Still, his ears were laid back and he looked the rogue he was. 'I don't like you like that,' said Jenny. 'Nobody would. I mean, you don't do yourself justice. Never mind. On Saturday we all went fishing. And Bashful and Gamester went with us – we didn't take the car. And when we got to the river, we took them out of the shafts, took their harness off and let them graze and roll. It made a change for them...' Before she had finished, Adamant's ears were pricked. The horse was listening intently, and I am ready to swear that he understood. And he looked magnificent. But that was as far as it went – I was taking no more risks.

As we moved away, Delaney looked at Falcon.

'Seeing's believing, Superintendent.'

'Yes,' said Falcon, 'it is. Because of that, I shan't tell anyone. I've never been called a liar, except from the dock.'

On Tuesday morning, Mansel and Falcon left. The latter had brought no driver, so Mansel sat by his side and Carson followed behind. And that was the end of a visit which neither Jenny nor I will ever forget.

A few days later, again I drove my wife to The Ne'er-do-well Home. By her desire, I did not wait this time: but I came back at five o'clock.

As we were driving home–

'They're taking no new patients,' said Jenny. 'As soon as those there have gone, the Home will be closed.'

'I think that's best, my darling.'

'Yes, I'm afraid it is.'

She said no more at that time, but when I kissed her goodnight, she slid an arm round my neck and held me close.

'Rosemary's failing,' she whispered. 'Her heart has been broken twice over. Before very long they'll be together again.'

Jenny saw her twice more. And then, when October was old and the fall of the leaf was in, Sister Helena died in her sleep.

So the tragedy came to an end, and the curtain fell.

This Large Print Book, for people
who cannot read normal print,
is published under the auspices of

THE ULVERSCROFT FOUNDATION

... we hope you have enjoyed this book.
Please think for a moment about those
who have worse eyesight than you ...
and are unable to even read or enjoy
Large Print without great difficulty.

You can help them by sending a
donation, large or small, to:

**The Ulverscroft Foundation,
1, The Green, Bradgate Road,
Anstey, Leicestershire, LE7 7FU,
England.**
or request a copy of our brochure for
more details.

The Foundation will use all donations
to assist those people who are visually
impaired and need special attention
with medical research, diagnosis
and treatment.

Thank you very much for your help.